SOME FINE
DOG

SOME FINE DOG

Patti Sherlock

Holiday House / New York

This book is dedicated to George,
whom all dogs love

Copyright © 1992 by Patti Sherlock
All rights reserved
Printed in the United States of America
First Edition

Library of Congress Cataloging-in-Publication Data

Sherlock, Patti.
     Some fine dog / by Patti Sherlock.
        p.   cm.
     Summary: Twelve-year-old Terry, star soloist in his church choir,
considers doing something else with his time when he finds his dream
dog, who turns out to be expert at learning and performing tricks.
     ISBN 0-8234-0947-3
     [1. Dogs—Fiction. 2. Singing—Fiction.] I. Title.
PZ7.S54517So 1992
[Fic]—dc20
                                                          91-856
                                                           CIP
                                                           AC

ACKNOWLEDGMENTS

For good advice I would like to thank Lezlie Couch, Dr. Roger Brunt, Ronna Marwill, DeeDee Sihvonen, and William Brennan, S.J.

P. S.

CHAPTER ONE

I tore around the corner of the alley and stopped short. There he sat, behind the church. The prettiest dog I'd ever seen.

Hunger for a dog, always gnawing inside me, rose up in my chest. I stretched out my arms and whispered, "Pup."

He turned his head toward me. His ears stood up and he tilted his head to one side. Black hairs oozed over one eye like melted licorice.

"Terence!" Father Egan waved at me from the basement door. Father Egan had picked up from my mother the bad habit of calling me "Terence."

"I'm coming," I called, but Father Egan had already disappeared inside. I was almost late for choir practice, but I needed to tell the dog something. I eased toward him, hoping he wouldn't run away. He looked up at me, trusting.

"Don't go anywhere," I said. "I'll be out in two hours." I stroked his head. "Stick around." When I got to the door I turned and said, "Stay here."

I hurried into the church basement. Father, his hands lifted in midair, stopped and looked at me. He was wearing his black coat and priest's collar.

A bad sign. On the days he wore flannel shirts, he acted more like a regular guy.

He pulled his wrist out of his black sleeve and looked at his watch. "Mr. Riley, what time is it?"

I shrugged.

"It is four minutes after four. What time does practice begin, Mr. Riley?"

"Four o'clock, Father."

He widened his eyes. "Did Our Lady of the Snows Boys Choir get its reputation by allowing tardiness?"

"No, Father." My voice sounded high, like one of the little boy's.

"Or mediocrity?"

"No, Father." My words stuck, and I had to swallow halfway through them. I started to move toward my row.

Father Egan leaned forward on his toes. "How *did* our Lady of the Snows Boys Choir get its reputation?"

Brad Anderson, a Protestant kid from Redbud, shot up his hand.

"Hard work and dedication!" he shouted.

Father Egan smiled. "Yes. Take your place, Terence." He tapped on his music stand. "We'll continue with our diction."

Every day we practiced pronouncing words. I wanted to sing the whole time, but Father Egan said too much singing would be a strain on young voices.

Derek Finlayson handed me a paper. *Daffodils*, it said on top. I remembered that poem from the year before. And the year before that and the year before that. I strained to see out the muddy basement window, wondering if the dog was still there.

"I wann-dered lone-lee as a clowwd," Father Egan began.

The rest of us joined in. ". . . that floats on high o'er vales and hills . . ."

"I saw a *croowd* . . ." Father Egan pointed to his own open, round mouth. "A host, of gol-den daff-oh-dils." I slipped a yawn in on the "oh."

When we finished reading the poem, Father Egan clasped his hands behind his back and began to pace. Even though he was short, no taller than us older boys, he seemed towering. Ma said even the bishop was scared of him.

"What do you think Wordsworth meant when he said that sometimes when he was in a thoughtful mood, a field of daffodils flashed upon the inward eye that is the bliss of solitude?"

Brad Anderson's hand shot up.

"I think he's saying he can see flowers when he closes his eyes."

Father Egan's forehead pulled into wrinkles. "Hm. Anyone else?"

My buddy Vic raised his hand.

"I think he's saying that if you have a neat time, nothin' can take it away from you."

I caught Vic's eye and pointed my thumb up.

Father Egan tilted his head. "What *would* take away someone's good times?"

Vic shrugged.

"Anyone?" Father Egan's eyes scanned the rows. The mine closing, I thought. I raised my hand. "Change. Stuff changes."

"Like?"

Stan, tall and skinny, answered.

"Like the guy who wrote this might move to a city or somethin'. And not be around fields of flowers no more. But he could remember 'em in his head."

Father Egan looked at the ceiling. "Yes." He peered at the bare light bulb for several moments. Then he picked up a yellowed sheet of music and waved it. "Shall we begin to sing?"

Mrs. North played a few measures of "An American Medley."

Father Egan crouched. He gathered in his arms and elbows. His old shoulders, bony under his coat, hunched forward.

We sucked in a big breath. Next moment, Father sprang up. He flung out his arms, and we began to sing.

Practice went fast after that. But I didn't forget for a minute the black-and-white dog in the alley.

When Father said a prayer at the end of practice, I couldn't concentrate on stuff like being grateful for the chance to serve God with songs. I only prayed the dog would still be there.

"Terence," Father Egan called to me as I left. "You will have a solo at the Fourth of July program. 'God Bless America.' "

"Okay," I answered.

I peered out the door. The dog was gone. My throat tightened.

"Terry!" Vic yelled at me as I dashed to the end of the alley to look down Main Street.

"Later!" I yelled back. Main Street was nearly deserted, like usual. I gazed north, to the end of the street where Main turned into a winding gravel road leading up to the mine, and then south, to the bridge over the river.

"Here, dog!" I called. "Here, boy!" If he'd found one of the roads leading to the foothills, he could be deep in the forest already. I sprinted down Silver Avenue, searching the alleys I passed.

Maybe someone else had picked him up. Anyone would want a dog that pretty.

I ran to the bridge and looked over. The North Fork was boiling with mountain runoff. The black-and-white dog was stealing up to a quiet place to get a drink.

"Hey, dog!" I yelled. The river drowned me out. "Don't move!" I hollered, and I ran to the end of the bridge and started down the steep banks.

The dog looked up and saw me coming. The sun, dropping toward the bare foothills and lumpy gray mining dumps, gleamed on his coat. He started toward me.

He didn't sidle or slink, like a nervous dog. He walked straight to me, looking up at my face. I dropped to one knee.

"Hi, boy."

He peered at me with big red-brown eyes.

"You lost?" I could hear the wishing in my voice. "Maybe I could take you home."

The dog sat down. He didn't wriggle and grin at the attention. He was friendly, but in a proud way. He leaned close against my knee, but peered off down Main Street.

"I might just show you to Ma . . ."

"No! No dog!" I could just hear her. We'd been over it all before. Still, this dog was real special.

I stood up and shaded my eyes. Something moved on the twisted road to the mine. Used to be, big trucks were always crawling up or down that road. I squinted, and saw it was only a security guard, as small as a mouse in that distance. That helped me remember that with the mine closed, we could hardly feed ourselves.

"C'mon, boy." I sighed. "I'll take you to Linda's. She's the Humane Society lady."

CHAPTER TWO

Without any coaxing, the dog walked beside me up the hill to Linda Baldwin's house.

Conrad, Linda's little fat kid, was chasing his sister around the yard with a rake.

"Knock it off, Conrad," I said. I reached for the white picket gate. But the dog jumped up on it with his front paws. The gate swung open and the dog, walking on his hind legs, pushed into the yard ahead of me. It was luck on the dog's part, but it looked real smart.

I tapped my knuckles on the screen door. "Your mom inside?" I asked. Conrad didn't answer. He looked at the dog and squinched up his eyes in a layer of fat. "*Another* one?" he asked.

"Hi, Terry." Linda pushed hair off her face and tucked it into her braid. She held the door open for me and the dog.

"A lost dog? Where'd you find him?"

"Behind the church. He's a border collie, isn't he?"

"Yeah. Somebody's probably worrying about this one."

Linda turned down the blaring TV and knelt

on the rug. I moved a stack of dog and cat magazines off a chair and sat down.

Linda ran her hands around the dog's white ruff, over his sleek black body, and down his white legs.

"Beautiful condition. No injuries. Young." She pulled back the dog's lips and looked at his teeth. She shook her head. "Pretty unusual for someone to lose track of a good border collie."

"How old is he?"

"Barely a year, I'd guess."

"But you haven't had any calls?"

Linda cocked her head and looked at me. "Terry, Maggie won't let you have him."

"Did I say I wanted him? I found a dog. He looked lost, so I brought him here. Okay?" I stopped. I didn't mean for my voice to get loud.

Linda blinked. She moved off her knees, stretched her legs onto the rug, and waved a housefly off the dog. She glanced at me, eyes full of pity.

"When the mine reopens, Terry . . ."

I wanted to stuff my ears. That's all anyone ever said. When the mine reopens we can pay the fuel bill. When the mine reopens we'll get new coats. When the mine reopens we can live like real people. I wanted to yell at Linda, *When will the mine reopen?*

Linda's husband, a tall, bony guy with long teeth and a skull-like head, was a manager at the mine. Shouldn't Linda know when the mine would reopen?

One of Linda's girls, sniffling from a fight, crawled onto her mother's lap. Linda petted the girl's head absentmindedly, like she would a dog.

I picked a cloth gingerbread man off the floor and put it on the little girl's knee. It was silly of me to feel mad at Linda. No one ever associated Linda with her husband and the mine. Everybody just knew her as the soft-hearted person who took in stray dogs and cats because the town was too small and too poor to have an animal shelter.

"How many animals you got these days?" I asked.

Linda wet her knuckles with her tongue, like a cat, and began to wash her little girl's face.

"No dogs right now, thank heavens. Four kittens, though."

"Will you be able to find homes for them?"

I'd made her feel bad again. Her eyes got misty. She hated it when she had to have Doc Brower put down animals because she couldn't find homes for them. She did more of that these days, since people couldn't afford pets.

I changed the subject. "What do you think of this dog?"

"He's pretty."

"Does he seem . . . is there something, I don't know, special about him?"

Linda threw back her head and laughed.

"In your eyes, they're all special. You thought the mutt I had here two weeks ago was outstanding at catching a ball. You thought the yellow Lab had great strength. The black cocker was really good with my children, you said. I shouldn't let you hang around here, torturing yourself over dogs."

I looked at the scuffed toes on my boots. My face felt hot.

Linda reined in her smile and made her face sober.

"You're right, though. There is something about this dog. He's confident and poised. Beautiful eyes. I bet he's really smart. Border collies can have remarkable minds."

"If you don't get a call from his owner, will you put him up for adoption?" I asked.

I didn't want her to look at me like she did, her forehead wrinkling up with sympathy.

"Terry, forget this dog. I'll hear from his owner. Besides, he's not the dog for you, even if Maggie would let you have one. A dozen ranchers would take him in a minute. Look at him, how bright he is. And just the right age to be a real help in herding livestock. It's in his blood, to be a working dog. He wouldn't be happy doing anything else."

I heard Linda's words in a back compartment of my brain. But I was looking into that black-and-white face and the large red-brown eyes that seemed to say, "I choose *you*."

Next day I tore out of choir practice. I ran to the church's front yard, looked down at the town, and breathed the thin June air. It prickled my nose.

My cowboy boots clicked like tap shoes going down the three flights of rock stairs to the sidewalk.

"Come in, Terry," Linda called from her living room before I even knocked.

"How did you kn—"

"How did I know it was you! Get serious. Did you fly over here? Choir practice couldn't have finished five seconds ago. Let's see . . . can I further demonstrate my psychic powers?" Linda closed her eyes and held her palm above them. "The boy wants to know, Has the border collie's owner contacted me?"

"Has he?"

"No."

"If it's somebody from the ranches in the valley, he should have called by now."

"True."

"Maybe the dog doesn't belong to anybody around here."

"I've been wondering about that myself. Maybe he fell out of a visitor's truck. Or maybe his owner drove off without him, thinking he was in the truck bed."

"Maybe someone tried to steal him, and he escaped."

Linda shrugged. "It's a puzzle."

I pushed a toy tractor with my toe.

"I guess I could just take him home and see what Ma says."

"Terry!" Linda moaned. "You know what the answer will be. How can you get your hopes up like this."

"Because I really want this one. More than I've wanted any of the others. And I think if I don't get him, I'll never find another one like him."

Linda raised her hands, palms open. "It's hard for your mother, Terry, with your dad away working odd jobs."

It's hard for me too, I thought. Every other summer, Dad's been here to go fishing and hiking with me. But if I had a dog . . . "At least I'm going to try," I said.

"Don't involve me in any way. Agreed?"

"Got it."

I stopped in the alley behind her house. Linda stood on her porch step, watching me go.

"I may be back," I mumbled.

CHAPTER THREE

Ma was facing the counter, rolling out dough, when I walked into the kitchen.

"Terence. You're late," she said. She started cutting the dough into strips without turning around.

"Oh boy, homemade noodles," I said. I'd have to play it just right. There was plenty against me keeping the dog, like our family being so poor right now. But I had a couple of things going for me. For one, Ma loved dogs. For another, she liked me to be happy. Ma thudded to the sink, scratching flour off her arms.

"They had a special on chicken at Broman's and I thought, 'How long has it been since I fed Terence chicken and nood—' What's that behind you, Terence?"

"Da-dum!" I jumped aside. "It's a dog, Ma." The border collie trotted over to her.

She made her eyes round. "Ah, so that's what it is. But what's it doing in my kitchen, Terence?"

"Linda Baldwin sent him over for us." I broke my promise not to drag Linda into it and told a lie all in one breath. I really wanted this dog.

"She says we need a watchdog with Dad working out of town."

The dog sniffed the linoleum floor, found a glob of flour, and licked it up.

"Terence Michael! You know we can't afford to feed a dog and give it shots and take it to the vet when it gets sick. We're doing good to keep bread on our table."

"When the mine reopens . . ."

"When the mine reopens, your dad will be home and we won't need a watchdog."

"We'll need one even more. Riffraff might be moving into town." I said "riffraff" like Ma did, with my nose wrinkled. Ma disliked "riffraff" almost as much as she admired people who were "better class." We didn't know too many of those kind, not in a small Idaho mining town, but she was convinced "better class" people went by their full names, like Terence Michael.

"Haven't we been over this before, Terence? No dog! We can chew up our own shoes. With wear." She glanced sidelong at my feet. "Why are you wearing your boots? You're supposed to save them for church."

"My tennis shoes have holes in them," I mumbled.

"See? And your knees have patches and Lord knows how we'll afford a winter coat for you next fall."

"When the mine reopens . . ."

". . . we'll be catching up on bills for a year. Then we'll talk about a dog."

"Don't you think he's beautiful?"

A curtain moved across Ma's eyes, darkening her face.

"I'm not giving him a single look. Take him back to Linda's."

"What if I got a job to pay for his keep?"

"What job? Don't I run myself ragged trying to find odd jobs that pay almost nothing? There's no money in this town, Terence."

"What about the old widows on pensions? They still get checks. And they need their lawns mowed and grass raked and trash carried."

It was the wrong thing to say to Maggie Riley. She strode toward me, her eyebrows latched together. The dog ducked behind me to get out of her way.

"Okay!" I said. My own brows hooked into an angry line. "I'll take him back. Linda will have him put down, like the others."

Ma stopped, and blinked. "What others?"

"She's had to put down five dogs this spring. Couldn't find homes for them. And lots of kittens."

Ma, shoulders sagging a bit, returned to the counter and began to lift noodle strips with a spatula. She sneaked a look at the dog. He gave her a yearning look in return. "Poor Linda," she said.

Something in her voice encouraged me.

"Ma, watch him while I go change my shoes, okay?"

"Sure, Terence, I don't have four hundred better things to do than baby-sit stray dogs."

"I don't want him to be lonely," I called over my shoulder. I flattened myself against the living room wall and peered around the doorjamb. *Talk to him, Ma,* I urged silently. My fingers dug into my palms. Ma moved over to dangle her finger above the dog's nose. The dog stretched out his neck, begging her to touch him. "Nice dog," she whispered.

I lifted my face to the ceiling. *Make her fall for him. Please.*

"Poor doggie doesn't want to be put down," Ma cooed. I grinned and hit my thighs with my fists. But I only smiled a minute. Then I saw myself in the dark confessional Friday night.

"Bless me, Father, for I have sinned. I told my mother a lie."

"Terence, your mother has a lot of worries with the mine closed." Father Egan wouldn't even pretend he didn't know it was me on the other side of the screen. *"It's been hard for Maggie with your father gone. Pride in you keeps her going. You're twelve years old now. Don't let her down."*

I shuffled back to the kitchen. My mom was eyeing the dog.

"The trouble with dogs," she declared, "is they die young and break your heart."

"Fran didn't die until she was thirteen!" I protested.

"That was too young."

Ma, stealing glances at the dog, ran steaming water onto her rolling pin. I stared at the worn linoleum. There was too much silence in the room.

"Ma, Linda wasn't for sure . . . she'd have to have him put down. She might . . . could. . . find a home for him."

Ma straightened up. She strode toward me, shaking her fist.

"You ornery snot! You were trying to trick me. I ought to—"

Ma stopped, and looked at the dog. The dog thrust his head forward, studying first one of us, then the other.

"Take him back, Terence."

For a minute, I had dared to hope. Now the impossibility of it all swept over me. I couldn't have a normal life unless the mine reopened. If it never reopened, I'd never have another thing I wanted. Besides, it was now, this summer, I wanted a dog. I longed for one every hour I was awake. A dog to fill the empty place Dad had left. A dog to wag its tail and chase after balls and believe life was cheerful, even though every human face in town wore a sign that said *Hard Times*. I felt my shoulders droop. I ordered the wetness in my eyes to leave. "C'mon," I commanded the dog, and slapped open the screen door.

"Terry?" I turned to look at my mom. Misery added to the tiredness of her face.

"I wish . . ."

I nodded. I knew she was sorry. She was crazy about dogs. So was my dad. Doomed by my genes, I thought. Dog lovers hung from every branch of the family tree.

A thought stole into my head. I let the open door swing shut. Didn't I owe it to myself to try one final thing?

"C'mon," I urged the dog, trying to keep defeat in my voice. "C'mon . . . Duffy."

Ma started. "What did you call him?"

I shrugged. "I'd already named him. Duffy."

Her eyebrows lifted. "After my dad?"

"Yeah. After Grandpa."

Her mouth started to tremble. "Dad would have loved that dog."

I nodded. I knew what her next words would be. *Dad loved all dogs, and all dogs loved him. He could make friends with any dog.*

"Dad loved all dogs," Ma said. "All dogs loved him. He could make friends with the meanest ones."

I kept my head down, but peeked up at my mom's face. Her eyes were wet.

"Why Duffy, Terence?"

"I thought it suited him. He has a nice face, like Grandpa did."

Her mouth turned slushy as she remembered her dad, who really did have a nice face. The dog, though, looked more sober than Grandpa often had.

Ma leaned over and ran her fingers down the dog's nose.

"Duffy?" she said, her voice husky.

I kept silent, winding a frayed shirt thread around my finger.

Suddenly Ma squared her shoulders and thrust out her jaw.

"You've got a good point, Terence. A boy ought to have a dog."

I nodded, certain I'd never said that, but happy to agree with it.

"Can you really feed him? Can you get enough yard jobs?"

"I can, Ma, I promise."

"He's on trial. If he costs me a cent, he has to go."

I bobbed my head.

"He's here against my better judgment."

I nodded.

"And another thing. He can't interfere with choir. That's where your opportunity is. Your chance to end up with a better . . ." She stopped before she said *class*. ". . . life."

"Ma-aa. How could Duffy interfere with choir?"

She turned and thudded back to the stove.

I crashed through the door to the backyard, Duffy at my heels.

"Ya-hoo!" I leaped and turned a circle in mid-air. Duffy tried to catch me by my jeans.

"Duffy! Ya-hoo! Whoooo!" I fell onto the dog and rolled him on the ground.

"But you heard, didn't you? You gotta be good."

Duffy lay on his back, feet paddling above him. He stretched out his white neck and gazed behind him, to the greening foothills and the dust gray mining dumps. And beyond, to the melting mountains.

CHAPTER FOUR

Sun streaming through my faded bedroom curtains tried to wake me next morning. Something wet on my cheek finished the job. I opened one eye.

"Duffy!" The dog rested his muzzle on my pillow and slurped my cheek again. How could a day start better?

Ma was sitting at the kitchen table, holding a grocery receipt. I danced over the cold linoleum.

"Who wound you up?" she asked. Then she mumbled, "Bananas, seventy-three cents . . . cleanser, a dollar nine . . ."

"Ma, they don't make mistakes on your grocery bill. Why do you waste your time checking on them?"

"They do make mistakes. Last week they charged me two dollars for cereal that was on special for a dollar fifty."

Fifty-cent mistake, big deal, I wanted to say. But I knew that would bring a lecture on how every fifty cents counted with us scraping.

I dished up the oatmeal left in the pan. "Is there more after this?" I asked. "I'm starving."

Ma's face tightened. "Make yourself more. But only use a fourth-cup cereal. That box has to last until Friday."

With the evidence of hard times glaring at me, I volunteered to go job hunting that very morning.

"I'll try some widows, like Mrs. Empey," I said. "Mrs. Empey has a big lawn and a lot of trees."

Ma looked kind of sad. "When your dad was home, he kept up old Nellie Empey's yard with no thought of money."

"When the mine reopens, Ma . . ." I drummed the table with my spoon and grinned. Ma kissed my forehead and picked up the altar linens she'd ironed for the church. Before she left, she stopped to pet the dog.

"I suppose you'll put us over the edge into the poorhouse. But you really are a handsome thing."

Duffy cocked his head. He looked like a picture on a dog calendar.

Before going to Nellie Empey's, I decided to walk over to Spruce Street, where old Mrs. Schwartz lived. Her grass was long, and turning brown in spots. When I knocked on the door a voice hollered, "Come in!"

The door creaked when I pushed it open. Across the room Mrs. Schwartz, straw hair standing on end, looked up from the TV. She scowled.

"You didn't bring lunch!"

I looked around to see if she was talking to me. Sure enough, I was the only other person in the room.

"I'm old, and I need to eat early! If I don't get lunch on time, I get sick."

It was nine thirty in the morning. "I—" I started.

"What good does it do for them to send lunch if I've already had to fix it for myself?"

"I don't—"

"And why do they put apples in the salads?" She shook a crooked finger at me. "You tell me that."

"Who?" I asked.

"The people at the church, who send lunches to shut-ins," she barked. I remembered then that three times a week the Community Church sent out hot lunches to old and handicapped people. Vic's mom and my mom and others from the Catholic church sometimes helped cook.

"They *say* they're doing a service for the elderly, but then they put apples in the salad, and I'll tell you something. Old people don't have the teeth for apples. Tell 'em to leave those apples *out!*"

I began to back toward the door. If Mrs.

Schwartz didn't even approve of free meals, she'd be impossible to please if she paid for jobs. I hoped I could slip out without explaining why I had come. As I shut the door behind me she was still hollering, "It makes old people sick to wait for their meals. But do those people care about that? No, they don't care!" I walked back to our street.

I gazed over the hedge at Nellie Empey's yard. It was in pretty good shape, really. Maybe she didn't need help. Suddenly a bonnet appeared above the hedge. Next came Mrs. Empey's wrinkly face. She had to stretch to see over the bushes.

"Oh, my land, it's you, Terry." She laughed, so piercing it startled me. "You had your breakfast? I've got some warm cinnamon rolls."

"I've had breakfast, but I'd like a cinnamon roll," I answered.

"HeeHEE, heeHEE." Everybody said Mrs. Empey sounded like a chicken when she laughed. "Typical boy. Always hungry. HeeHEE, hee-HEE."

Mrs. Empey had a pie-shaped face, decorated with a thousand creases. "You come on in too, feller," she told Duffy. "I'll find a heel of bread for you."

As she poured me a glass of milk, I asked, "Do you have any yard work around here, Mrs. Empey?" I added, "I'm looking for a summer job," so she wouldn't think I was offering to do it for free, like Dad used to.

"My land, I had a notion to ask you, Terry, but I thought you were too busy with choir."

"Not so busy I can't do some work on the side," I said.

Mrs. Empey paused for a minute. Then she said, "You bet I'll hire you."

A grin stretched my face. I reached over and patted Duffy. But I had no idea how to bring up the subject of wages. Lucky for me, old Nellie even did that.

"Would you cut and rake the lawn, do the hedge, and haul trash away for five dollars a week?" she asked. "I'll set my own hoses and weed the flower beds. I'm old"—she nodded, like a chicken pecking—"but I'm not helpless."

"How about I start after lunch?" I asked. In the meantime, I'd play a bit with Duffy.

When I passed the church on my way home, I couldn't resist its grassy hillside. I rolled down it, spinning over and over. Duffy bounded after me, barking.

"Duffy! Five dollars a week! That's plenty for dog food. I'll even have money for extras, like a collar and a dog brush."

At home, I rummaged in the shed for Fran's

old toys. I found her pink ball, but it was so badly chewed that when I threw it, it only went a couple of feet.

Behind our garden tools, I found a red Frisbee I hadn't played with for a long time.

"Here," I told Duffy. "You know how to catch one of these?" I flung the Frisbee. Duffy watched it, ears perked, but he didn't move from where he was sitting.

"I guess you don't know how to play. Here . . ." I wiggled the Frisbee back and forth under Duffy's nose. He clamped his jaws on it.

"Okay, here goes." Duffy let go as I pulled back my arm. Duffy ran after the red toy. When it started to descend, Duffy leaped into the air.

"Wow! Caught it the first time!" I'd seen Frisbee dogs on TV and expected it took a long time to train them. Duffy trotted back to me with the Frisbee in his mouth.

"Give it to me!" I ordered.

I threw it again, harder. This time Duffy had to race, but by the time the Frisbee began to fall, the dog was under it.

I wondered if it was beginner's luck, or if Duffy really understood. I tossed the Frisbee in a different direction. A breeze caught it, and it sailed over the fence into the Abelsons' yard. Shoot, I thought, this might confuse him.

"We'll have to go around through the alley," I

told Duffy. There was no way to get over the Abelsons' fence and thick hedge. I started out our back gate and noticed Duffy wasn't with me. He was sitting below the hedge, gazing up at it. It was much too high to jump.

"C'mon," I called.

Duffy ran back and forth beside the row of bushes. At the end of the hedge, beside the shed, a ladder was propped. I watched, mouth open, while Duffy slowly climbed its rungs.

"That won't do any good." I laughed.

When Duffy reached the sixth rung, he jumped sideways, landed on top of the Abelsons' hedge, and jumped into their yard. I stared at where the dog had been.

"Well, I guess I'll go rescue him," I mumbled. There was no way for him to get back.

Just then a black-and-white form appeared on top of the hedge again. Duffy sailed into our yard, the Frisbee in his teeth.

"Duffy!" It sounded like a scolding. The dog's head ducked. "Good boy," I corrected myself.

I shoved a rusted hand mower through the grass at Mrs. Empey's. I couldn't stand to go so slow. I leaned into the mower and forced it to run across the lawn.

The smell of cut grass mingled with a pine scent floating down from the peaks. Duffy trotted beside me. Why, I wondered, did I feel funny about Duffy figuring out how to get over the fence for the Frisbee? I wanted a smart dog, didn't I?

I threw the mower handle back and headed the other direction. I saw a dark-haired kid at the end of the block.

"Vic!" I called.

Vic trotted up the street, holding three trout on a willow limb.

"Hey, nice," I said. "You get 'em at the river?"

"Yep. What the heck are you doing?"

"Cutting Mrs. Empey's grass."

Vic shook his head. "What a Boy Scout."

"You seen my dog yet?" I stepped aside to give Vic a view of Duffy. I waited for his compliment.

"I can't believe your mom let you keep him."

"I'm paying his way."

A white head leaned around the old stone house's front door.

"HeeHEE, heeHEE," cackled Mrs. Empey. Her chicken laugh could be heard blocks away. "Don't this lawn look better?" she called. "How do, Vic?"

"Fine." Vic smiled.

"Terry, when you're done, could you empty the duck pond in the backyard and then give Curly and Donald fresh water?"

"Sure."

"HeeHEE. Ain't it nice to have a hired man around?" The white head disappeared inside.

"Hi, Tewwy." I looked over and saw Conrad, Linda's chubby boy, and three of his friends.

"Hey, your mom know you're out of the yard?"

Conrad's jaw protruded. "Yeth! She thaid I could go up to Leo's."

Duffy, lying beside the stone border, perked his ears. He crept onto the sidewalk. The boys, led by a waddling Conrad, trooped past Vic and me. Leo, a sandy-haired kid, reached out and tapped Duffy on the nose. Duffy tolerated the petting, then slunk a few feet away. He positioned himself in front of the group, ears flickering.

Conrad stepped forward, slowly.

"Does he bite?" he asked.

"What's that dog doing?" Vic whispered.

I shrugged.

Duffy dropped to his stomach. His head thrust forward. He rested his head on his front paws and gazed solemnly at the little boys.

Conrad began to walk backward. Duffy ran in a half crouch until he had circled behind the boy. Eyes intent, he dropped again to his stomach.

Linda's words came back to me. "It's in his blood to be a working dog." Sure, that was it. He was trying to herd the boys, like he would cattle or sheep.

"Hey." I laughed. The dog had worried me for a minute, looking so intense. "Let those guys go, Duffy."

Duffy trotted right to me.

"Can't you tell the difference between little kids and sheep?" I asked him. Duffy gazed at me, his red-brown eyes serious.

Vic finally had a comment on my new dog. "He's weird," he said.

When Vic came by later to pick me up for choir practice, I found a big rope to tie to the collar I'd bought for Duffy. "I don't want him getting into trouble," I told Vic. I weighed the thick rope in my hand. "A dog tied with this can't get loose."

CHAPTER FIVE

Vic raced me to the church. I took the lead, but he was breathing down my collar.

"Can Riley," I puffed, "the champion in holey sneakers from Silverbow, Idaho, keep his title? Or will DeFazio, the challenger, give him the race of his *life?*"

On Lode Street, I tore downhill. The church spire rose up into blue sky, matching in shape the peaks behind it.

I reached the basement door a step before Vic. We burst in. Father Egan, wearing a brown flannel shirt, was bent over the piano, talking with Mrs. North. "We're on time," I panted, and shoved Vic ahead of me to his row.

"Hey," hissed Brad Anderson, the Protestant kid from Redbud. "How come Father Egan sometimes wears his black priest's clothes and sometimes he just wears regular shirts?"

I turned around to answer him. "Holy days," I said solemnly. "When he's got on his black stuff and collar, you know it's a holy day." Vic glanced toward me and grinned wickedly.

I went on, with a straight face. "On holy days, you need to be real reverent, Anderson." Brad bobbed his head, his mouth open. I had to stare at my diction sheet to keep from laughing.

It wasn't so much that we didn't like Anderson. It was his mom. She drove him the fifteen-mile trip from Redbud every day, even in winter, when nobody in his right mind would risk that twisting road. Half the time she sat in on choir practice, reading a book but looking up and beaming at us when we sang.

Our choir had all kinds of kids in it. Tall ones, with splotchy, teenage faces, and short ones, with round, little-kid faces. We were curly headed and straight, neat and sloppy, town kids and ranch kids. But when we sang together, something great came out.

Every year somebody spread rumors that Father Egan had an offer from some big church in a city or a Catholic college somewhere. But he stayed on in Silverbow. Dad said he liked working in an isolated Rocky Mountain town where there weren't many activities to distract kids from joining the choir. In Silverbow, there was only football when you got to high school, and Our Lady of the Snows Boys Choir before that.

Father Egan lifted his arms, and we began. In a moment he screamed "Stop!" and buried his face in his hands, like he was crying. But we were used to that. For most of the practice, he seemed in a great mood.

"Pass your music to the end of the rows." Father Egan wore a sly grin.

I leaned around to look at the basement clock. It said seven minutes to six.

"What's going on?" Anderson whispered. "He never ends practice early."

Father Egan announced, "We'll use our last few minutes today to talk about our summer engagements." He tilted his head and smiled. "We're going to be busy.

"You know about the Fourth of July concert in the park. We'll be the only attraction this year, because the town has no money for fireworks."

"No fireworks?" moaned Danny, a fourth grader.

"Then, on July 10, we'll go by bus to Boise and sing at the dedication of the new St. Catherine's Church. On July 21, we'll sing for a business convention in Twin Falls. That's a paid appearance. Profits will go into the scholarship fund.

"On August 3, we have another paid engagement. In Helena, Montana. And on August 10"— Father Egan ran his hand through his sparse hair—"the choir will sing for something very . . . special . . . to me." His lips pulled back over yellowed teeth into an uneven grin.

"It will be the fiftieth anniversary of my ordination to the priesthood."

Everybody applauded. "Clap!" Anderson said,
smacking my shoulder.

Father Egan flushed. "Priests from across the
state, and the bishop, will be here. There will be
a dinner and a luncheon, but most important, of
course, will be the Mass and the music of the
choir. We'll start our new music this week; some
of it is difficult."

Father Egan's lips still turned up in a smile.
"All right, boys, that's it. See you tomorrow."

I tried to shove past Brad Anderson, who had
crowded in front of me.

"Terence," Father Egan called. "Stay where
you are. I need to talk to you."

I looked at Vic and shrugged.

After the room was empty, Father Egan took
me by the shoulder and steered me toward a
chair.

"Terence. For the anniversary celebration,
you'll do a solo. The 'Ave Maria.' "

"Okay." I loved the "Ave Maria," the famous
song to the Mother of Jesus.

"You'll need to schedule extra practice time
with Mrs. North." Father Egan smiled toward
Julia North.

"Julia, I think Terence's solo will be the high
point. Even those who've heard the choir in pre-

vious years won't expect us to have a soloist like him."

Mrs. North nodded her gray head and beamed at me.

"I tell you, Terence, when they hear you do the 'Ave' "—Father Egan turned his face toward the light bulb—"they'll think an angel from heaven has come to earth to sing."

Vic was waiting for me on the steps. We ambled home beside the river. High water from snow melting in the mountains crashed over the rocks.

"I wonder if we'll have the bus driver with the hairy arms again," Vic said.

"Huh?"

"For the out-of-town trips. Father Egan was mad at him last summer, because he cussed so bad. I wonder if we'll get to go to the water slide in Boise."

"I dunno."

"Anyway, I know what the highlight of *my* summer will be." Vic lifted his chin and put his hand on his heart. "When Terence Riley sings the 'Ave,' it will be like an angel from heaven has—"

"Spy!"

"I was waiting for you! I couldn't help overhearing."

We turned onto my street. Suddenly Vic

stopped. I followed his gaze up the hill. "Uh-oh,"
I muttered.

"See ya." Vic swung off into the alley.

Ma stood by the front gate, a fist on one hip.
Her other hand held a short piece of chewed-up
rope, with Duffy tied at the end of it. Duffy
peered mournfully down the hill at me.

I felt like I was wading through tar, climbing
that hill.

"Hi, Ma."

She shoved the rope at me.

"Here. Your dog. He killed old Nellie Empey's
ducks."

CHAPTER SIX

"The only thing old Nellie had left in the world was those ducks." Ma's voice cracked. "She and her husband brought them to town with them when they sold their farm. What are you going to do about this, Terence?"

I stared at my shoes, not answering.

"I'll tell you what you're going to do. You go over, apologize, and tell her you'll pay for those ducks." Ma slapped a tear off her cheek. "Even though money can't really repay poor Nellie."

I tied Duffy's stubby rope to a tree in Nellie's yard, then climbed the porch and waited, trying to find courage to knock.

"Nellie. I'm sorry about your ducks," I rehearsed. "And I'll be happy to work off the cost of them." That wasn't quite true, because then I'd have no money for dog food. And that meant getting rid of Duffy.

I rapped softly, hoping she wouldn't hear me. To my surprise, the door swung open.

"Come in," Nellie called. She turned and started down the dark hallway, rocking lopsidedly on her arthritic legs. I cast a look back at Duffy. His ears hung limp.

The hall smelled dank, like forest places where sunlight doesn't reach. But the kitchen was sunny, and fragrant from a pot boiling on the stove.

"You'll have a cookie, won't you, boy?" I heard strain in Nellie's voice.

"No thanks."

She turned and looked at me sharply.

"You sick?"

"Sort of. Mrs. Empey, I'm awful sorry about Donald and Curly."

She limped over to me and peered straight up into my eyes.

"I know." Then she shocked me.

"HeeHEE, heeHEE," she cackled, so loud I jumped. "I told your mama it didn't matter, but she was in a tizzy and wouldn't listen."

Nellie leaned close, tilting her head. "I hated them ducks. *Hated* 'em."

"But they were all you had left from . . ."

"Sure! And they should have stayed on the farm where they belonged. Even there, I hated 'em. Nasty things. Terry, there's nothing any dirtier 'n a duck. I told old Bob Empey, 'We can't take them ducks to town with us. There's a law agin 'em.' But old Bob, he went to the mayor's house and talked to him. And the mayor said, 'You bet you and Nellie can bring your pet ducks with you. Just keep 'em in the backyard.' "

"But after your husband died . . ."

"You think I was going to kill 'em? And have that old man come back to haunt me? HUH!"

Nellie thrust her hand into a ceramic pig cookie jar.

"Sit down!"

I pulled out a metal chair with a patched cloth seat.

"They should have died years ago. Never heard of ducks living so long. I think they kept agoin' just to spite me." She poured a glass of milk from a quart carton. "And your dog, bless his heart, he didn't mean to kill 'em."

"What happened?"

"Duffy ran past my house, dragging his rope, looking for you, I suspect. I called to him, and he remembered me. Came right over. I grabbed the rope and took him to the backyard with me while I was changing the hoses.

"Suddenly, he spied them ducks. He crouched down real low"—Nellie lowered her already stooped back and began to creep around the table—"and when the ducks began to squawk and flap, he broke away from me. Then he ran around them ducks in a circle.

"They'd dash this way . . . so would he. They'd dash that way. He'd cut 'em off. HeeHEE. I wish you could've seen 'em." Nellie straightened. "That dog had me laughing so hard, I thought my old heart would give out." Her wrinkled face pulled into pleats around her mouth.

"It was a big game for all of 'em. And then, all of a sudden, Donald flopped over. I went over and picked him up, and saw he'd played himself to death. I cleaned and dressed him quick and put him in the pot. Curly, he didn't look so good either, so I chopped off his head and put 'im in with his friend. I thought he'd want it that way. HeeHEE, heeHEE!" Her chicken laugh rang off the walls and floated out the open window.

"Are they . . . I mean, is that what smells so good?"

"You bet! Duck soup. HeeHEE." She wiped her eyes with the back of her hand. "What are we going to do about your mama? She thought I was just saying it, when I told her it was all right."

I shrugged.

"Maybe we better go ahead and settle up, so she'll be happy."

"Oh, sure." I hoped I didn't look too startled. Nellie had seemed so cheerful about the accident, I'd thought there wasn't going to be any talk of payment.

I gulped. "How much are ducks worth?"

"You can get ducks for a song." Her eyes disappeared in wrinkles and her lips pulled tight over her chipped teeth.

I nodded, confused. She thrust her head forward and cocked it, like a hen.

"Terry Riley, you can sing me a song."

"Yeah?"

"Do you know 'Red River Valley'?"

"No. Maybe Father does. I could ask . . ."

"Sure, he'll know it. It goes:

From this valley they say you are going,
We will miss your bright eyes and sweet smile.
For they say you are taking the sunshine
That has brightened my pathway awhile.

I tried not to scrunch up my face. Nellie Empey sang awful.

Come and sit by my side if you love me,
Do not hasten to bid me adieu . . .

"Anyway, you get the padre to teach it to you. And then come over and sing it for me. And that'll buy two old ducks."

"Sure." Relief swept over me and I took a swig of milk. Nellie tapped my uneaten cookies with her crooked old finger.

"Eat up, Terry." She eased herself into the chair across from me. "You need to know that song anyway. So someday you can sing it to a pretty girl." Nellie looked out the window, but I don't think she was seeing anything. She was staring at memories inside her head. I wondered, Was it old man Empey, the friend of messy ducks, who used to sing that song to her?

When I left Nellie's, I decided to go to Linda's house instead of straight home. I wanted to give Ma more time to cool off.

Linda was weeding her vegetable garden. She stood up, dusted off her knees, and shook her head at Duffy and his chewed-up rope.

"Maggie told me what happened," she said.

"What am I going to do about him?"

She looked at me a long time. Then she answered, "Maybe it's not too late to find this dog a home on a ranch."

I jerked Duffy over to me. I must have scowled awful because Linda looked startled.

"Or, if you're determined to keep him—"

"I am!"

". . . then you're going to have to get a chain to tie him. It's obvious he'll chew through any rope. I'll loan you one for the time being. And, you'll have to make him think he's useful. Make him think he has a job. You can start by letting him bring in the paper—"

"We don't take the paper anymore."

"The mail, then." Duffy sat on the sidewalk, leaning against Linda's leg and scrutinizing her with his red-brown eyes. "But that won't be enough for this dog.

"Hey!" she said. "I think I have a book somewhere on training trick dogs. Maybe you could teach him tricks, and he'd feel like he was working."

"Are tricks hard to teach?"

"You need to be consistent, work with the dog every day. Let me see if I can find that book. Keep an eye on these kids."

Linda was back in a minute with *How to Train the Trick Dog.* "I haven't looked at this in years. If I remember right, it's a step-by-step method. You start with simple tricks, build on them, and by the book's end, you're doing pretty impressive stuff."

"Will I need any special equipment?"

"You have most of the things you need—a stool, cans, a wheelbarrow. You'll need to have something around for rewards—dog biscuits or a food he likes."

"Hey, look. 'Jumping Through a Hoop.' "

"Don't start with anything that advanced. Start with shaking hands."

"This guy in the picture doesn't have a hoop. He has a broom handle."

"I remember that one. You start by asking the dog to jump over a stick . . ."

Linda walked over and picked up a long twig. She held it low to the ground. "You call the dog. . . . Here, Duffy."

Duffy perked his ears and hopped over the twig to get to Linda.

"As the days go on, you hold the stick higher. When the dog gets used to jumping over the stick, you replace the stick with a hoop."

"Try it higher; see what he does."

"We don't have any treats for him. But . . . well, let's try it just a little higher."

Linda moved away, holding the stick. "Duf—" she began, but the dog leaped over the twig before she finished his name. He sat down beside her, peering up at her face with earnest eyes.

"Wow." Linda grinned at me. "This dog really wants to please. Conrad, go get Mommy a dog biscuit from under the kitchen sink."

Duffy's eyes didn't leave Linda's face. She shook her head. "Shall we try it higher?" Linda lifted the stick so it was level with her waist.

"Over, Duffy."

The dog sailed over the stick and sat down

beside Linda, his tail blanketing her toes, eyes intent on her face.

Linda took the dog biscuit from Conrad and gave it to Duffy.

"Terry, this dog is sharp. I'd almost suggest . . ." She stopped. "Never mind, it's too short notice."

"What?"

"I was thinking if you could develop a dog act with Duffy, I'd hire you to entertain at Steffie's birthday party."

"Sure! We could."

"It's only nine days from now, and that's really not enough time to—"

"You see how quick he learns."

"But you have choir, and Nellie's yard to keep up."

"Linda, please? If it looks like Duffy can't be ready, I'll let you know a few days ahead so you'll have time to plan games or something."

Linda pushed her index finger against her lower lip and looked at the dog. She shrugged. "I guess you can try." She laid her hand on Duffy's head. "I'll be a little jealous of you, Terry, working with a dog like this. He seems to read people's minds."

I grabbed Duffy's gnawed-up rope and the book and hurried out the gate. "Thanks!" I hollered back.

I wasn't reluctant to go home now. Linda didn't

realize what she'd done for me. Ma was going to point out that Duffy was off to a bad start, and the next time he got in trouble it might cost us plenty.

But I could argue that Duffy was an opportunity the Riley family badly needed. Because I could earn money with him. Duffy and I were going to be entertainers.

CHAPTER SEVEN

I opened the dog-training guide to Chapter One, "How to Get Started." Studying a book wasn't my idea of summer fun. But Linda had said it was important that I read it from beginning to end. "If you don't know what you're doing, you could ruin Duffy," she'd told me.

Right off, the book warned that dog training could be aggravating, and that a handler should never scold or hit a dog. That seemed pretty obvious to me.

The second chapter talked about "natural tricks" like sneezing and yawning. If you could catch a dog doing some normal action, like scratching, tell him "Scratch!" and give him a treat, pretty soon the dog would be scratching on command. I skimmed those pages, wanting to get to the *real* tricks.

Chapter Three told about famous dogs in history. I fell asleep.

When Ma came home and slammed the kitchen door, I woke up. I picked up the book again. Chapter Four got into useful stuff, like the equipment I would need: a bucket or stool to use for a platform, a six-foot lightweight rope, and maybe a choke collar.

"Terence! You've got a half hour until choir practice," Ma called. "Have you showered?"

"I'm not dirty," I called back. That wasn't exactly true, but I'd just reached an interesting part, about rewards. Dogs who loved to eat were easier to train, the book said. That was good news, because Duffy was always sniffing around the kitchen, begging Ma for stuff. And when she gave him any scrap, even a piece of moldy bread, he'd bolt it down like it was steak.

The author liked to use cut-up hot dogs for treats, because dogs love the flavor. I made myself a note and stuck it in my shirt pocket, "Pick up hot dogs." I would have to hide the package in the back of the refrigerator, because Ma had stopped buying hot dogs a year before. They weren't a good value, she said. She would have a fit if I bought Duffy treats we couldn't afford for ourselves.

I stole a few more minutes to read about the trick called "Go to Place." It was the basis for all other tricks. Working an hour a day, I'd be able to train Duffy to do a trick a week. A week! How could I have a whole act ready for Steffie Baldwin's birthday party, only eight days away, if one trick took a week to teach?

On the way home from choir, I stopped at Broman's. Mr. Broman, an old guy in a smudged shirt whose eyeglasses were held together at the side with a paper clip, was stocking tomatoes in a bin. I walked up to him before I lost my nerve.

"Could I charge a package of hot dogs until next Friday?" I asked. His eyebrows flew up. Ma liked to brag, in front of Mr. Broman sometimes, that no matter how poor we got, she never charged her groceries. She said that was like asking for charity.

Mr. Broman took off his glasses and looked at me. "Sure, Terence. Don't ever hesitate to ask me if you need something from my store."

Mr. Broman thought the hot dogs were for me. Well, in a way, they were. I had to get started training and I'd already spent my first week's wages on a small sack of dog food and a collar. As it was, I lacked the other stuff the book said I needed. My search of the shed hadn't turned up any lightweight rope, and I didn't have a choke collar either.

At supper, Ma looked down at Duffy, whose eyes were begging, and said, "So, dog, when are you going to make us rich?" She sent a crooked smile my way.

"I never said *rich,* Ma."

"You said rich, Terence."

"I said Duffy might be able to help out."

"Oh, it's help out now, huh?" Ma held out a

pork chop bone and looked Duffy right in the eye. "You don't have to help out, or make us rich. Just stay out of trouble and don't make us poorer."

I picked up an old bucket from the shed and headed for Miner's Park on the edge of town. Duffy wove around my legs, nearly tripping me. I think he smelled the hot dog in my shirt pocket.

Mount Columbine's head jutted up from a collar of white clouds. The valley's farmers had just mowed alfalfa, and the evening was heavy with scent.

"Now, Duffy, we're going to go slow," I told him. I'd skipped the commands "Come" and "Sit" because Duffy already seemed to understand those words. I wanted to jump ahead to Chapter Ten, "Developing a Dog Act," but I forced myself to find the page for "Go to Place."

I turned our rusted metal bucket upside down. I would find a scrap of carpet to tack onto it, and it would be my makeshift platform. To get the dog on top of the platform, the book said I should push him with my left hand and pull on his leash with my right hand. I read the instructions three times. Even if I'd had a leash, I wouldn't have understood what I was supposed to do.

Finally I turned to Duffy, patted the platform, and said, "Get up here, boy." He astonished me by jumping right onto the bucket. Of course, he jumped right off again.

I turned to the page explaining how to teach "Stay." I told Duffy, "Get back up here," placed my hand in front of his nose, and said, "Duffy. Stay." When he did, I praised him. At first, he wanted to jump off and sit on my foot more than he wanted to stay on the platform, but it only took about ten corrections to convince him he had to stay on the bucket until I said it was okay to leave.

"Hey, you're something!" I shook Duffy's paw. I sat down in the grass and hugged him. Duffy tucked his muzzle under my chin. The book had said "Go to Place" would take a week to teach, but Duffy seemed to have it down already.

Duffy snuggled closer to me. "You lovin' dog," I said. Just then, he snatched the hot dog from my shirt pocket, ran out of reach, and downed it in one gulp.

"Hey! You tricked me." Duffy, licking his lips, ducked his head.

"It's okay," I told him. "It was for you anyway."

He trotted back and cuddled up to my chest, though I had no more hot dogs for him to snitch.

Next day after dinner I told Ma, "I'm going to the park to play Frisbee with Duffy."

"Do you have any songs you need to practice?"

"No!" I said.

"Your chores at Nellie's all done?"

"Yes."

I'd left my bucket platform in the weeds at the park. I didn't want to make too much of my dog training around Ma. She was so touchy about choir coming first in my life.

To avoid telling a lie, I made it a point that night, and all the following ones, to start my training session with a Frisbee game. Duffy now made such spectacular catches that he sometimes drew an audience from people walking or driving past.

A couple of times Vic came by. He thought training was boring, but he loved to throw the Frisbee for Duffy. He made such hard throws Duffy sometimes had to spiral in the air or make fantastic leaps to catch it.

"Man, doesn't he ever get tired?" Vic asked one night. Sweat was rolling down his cheeks.

"I can't wear him out," I said. "Maybe that's because he's a working dog."

I never felt any frustration teaching tricks, the way the book had warned I might. I only felt amazement that Duffy could understand so quickly what I wanted from him. I had started to hatch big ideas about my dog act—performing for the governor, stuff like that—when two things happened.

One night, as Duffy and I were leaving the

park, a small plane buzzed overhead, getting ready to land on the dirt strip beyond the weed fields. I watched as the pilot circled.

"Neat plane, huh, boy? Probably bringing in fishermen."

Suddenly I realized Duffy wasn't beside me. He was running under the plane, barking up at it.

"Duffy! *Come back!*" I screamed. I could picture him sliced to ribbons by the propeller when the plane put down.

"Duffy!" I screamed. Either he couldn't hear me because of the engine noise, or he was ignoring me.

The plane landed, just ahead of Duffy, with Duffy still chasing it. I was terrified Duffy would reach the plane while the propeller was still spinning. My stomach lurched and a sour taste sloshed up into my throat.

Then something strange happened. As soon as the plane began to taxi to a stop, Duffy dropped to his stomach and gave the plane "the eye."

I could see faces staring out the cockpit. I suppose the passengers thought they were seeing a mad dog. It was crazy, on his part, to think he could herd a plane.

In the other incident, I didn't feel upset or scared—just sad.

Duffy and I were heading to the park one night after dinner. Duffy was dancing, excited to start catching the Frisbee, when a semi-truck pulling a big stock trailer passed us. Duffy turned at the noise of sheep blatting. I sniffed the air—it smelled like ammonia and wet wool. The truck's license plate read CALIFORNIA. I figured the truck must be bringing sheep up from California for summer grazing in our mountains. Forest rangers counted sheep going onto forest allotments at the loading corrals outside of town.

Duffy looked at me, then started to trot after the truck. I didn't call him back—I was curious myself to go watch the men unload sheep.

The truck driver was baked dark brown and had a narrow mustache. He looked at the loading chutes, shouted in a foreign language, then pulled open the trailer gate.

Sheep, making a huge racket, poured down the ramp. When one ewe in front reached the opening to the sorting corral, she balked and tried to turn around. Twenty sheep pressed up behind her.

Duffy sped across the empty field and leaped onto the balky sheep's back.

"Duffy! No! Bad dog!" I yelled. He couldn't hear me above the commotion.

As soon as the ewe felt Duffy on her back, she

bolted through the gate. With Duffy still riding her neck, the ewe tore down the chute's alleyway. A stream of sheep poured after her.

The man with the thin mustache looked over at me. His face was a dark storm, but he clasped his hands together and waved them above his head. It looked like he meant "thank you."

After the lead sheep moved, Duffy jumped off and scanned the area. Some ewes were milling on the ramp, causing a bottleneck. Duffy streaked to the fence, jumped it, and leaped onto another sheep's back. The sheep trotted down the ramp.

The dark man pointed at the dog, pointed at his own head, and nodded excitedly. I thought it might be rude to call Duffy then. So I walked over to the park by myself, sat down on a bench, and avoided looking over to the corrals. After a few minutes, I felt Duffy's head under my hand. His fur was hot.

"Do you think you're ready to do some training now?" I asked.

Duffy gazed at me with red-brown eyes.

I plunked the bucket upside down. "Go to place!" I ordered. Duffy jumped obediently onto his platform. "Stay," I commanded. Duffy didn't try to leave. But every once in a while he swiveled his head around to peek at the column of dust where forest rangers were counting sheep.

CHAPTER EIGHT

On the Fourth of July, I hurried home from the picnic as soon as I finished singing "God Bless America." I wanted to run through Duffy's routine. Steffie Baldwin's birthday party was the next day and I hoped to amaze Linda.

"Duffy!" I moaned when I opened the gate. I had chained Duffy far from Ma's flowers, but he had managed to pull the chain taut, stretch out his paws, and dig. Dying flowers—yellow daisies, orange marigolds, and blue pansies—were strewn everywhere.

Ma would be furious. "My flowers," she often said, "are my tranquilizers. When I'm working in the garden, I don't worry about our bills."

Last summer, before the mine had shut down, word had come to town one afternoon that there'd been an accident at the mine. Ma went right outside, knelt among the tulips, and pulled weeds. She'd stayed there until Dad, unharmed, walked through the front gate.

I yanked Duffy's chain. "Bad dog!" I scolded. Duffy, who had been wagging his hind end off, looked at me, shocked. Then he bowed his head and slunk away.

"Do you always need to be . . . *doing* something?" I cried. "Why can't you just sleep and eat, like other dogs?"

With my hands, I began to push dirt back into the gulches Duffy had made. I picked up a daisy. It drooped over my thumb. Though it seemed a useless thing to do, I placed the flower back in the ground and mounded dirt around it. If I scooped all the dirt back into the holes and replanted the flowers, Ma might think they'd died of disease or something.

By the time I heard Ma coming up the street with her friend Louise, I'd replanted the withering plants approximately in their original locations. I loosed Duffy, moved to the other side of the yard, and tried to look casual. Ma strode up the walk without noticing the pitiful flowers.

"Terence Michael." Ma beamed. "You were wonderful!" She squeezed my shoulder. "Know what Father said? Told me it's almost certain you'll win the choir scholarship when you graduate." She leaned her head close. "Didn't I tell you?"

Our Lady of the Snows awarded a three-thousand-dollar scholarship every year to someone graduating from the choir. Boys graduated when their voices changed, about age thirteen or fourteen. The bank kept the money for the kid until he finished high school.

"An education for my boy." Ma wiggled the top of my ear. "And someday, a safe, dependable job."

"Ma, I've told you before. The scholarship is for someone who plans to study music in college. And I don't want to."

"So the beggar can be choosy, eh? You'll go to school however you can get there, Terence. If you have to major in music, you'll major in music."

Ma flicked my chest with her knuckles. "Hey, don't make a face. God gives you a beautiful voice and you want to waste it?"

"Ma, nobody knows what my voice will be like when it changes. Sometimes a guy doesn't have any voice at all after it deepens. Anyway, I may want to be a forest ranger or an archaeologist or something."

"You're too young to know what you want! By the time you're a senior in high school, you'll understand how it is in the real world. That people without money don't go to college, unless somebody sends 'em."

"I could get another kind of scholarship, like Benny Marrs did."

"Ha! Good example. Benny Marrs got straight *A*'s and wonderful scores on his college exams.

You know how much Benny's scholarship was?"

She sunk her finger into my chest. "Four hundred dollars a year. You know how far that goes at college? Benny had to drop out his second year, when the mine shut down. He goes to night school now."

Ma looked triumphant. Even though I knew how stubborn she could be, I tried once more.

"Ma, a lot of kids from Silverbow have gone to college without the choir scholarship."

"That was before the silver market crashed. Mining families can't help their kids anymore."

Ma, her chin out, watched me. I gazed over the fence, down the hill, at a row of houses with peeling paint.

"Besides," Ma said. "You go into music, you'll always be around better-class people."

"I want a choice."

Ma knotted her brows. "Choices, Mr. Think Big, are for rich people. The children of doctors and lawyers and politicians . . . they get to choose. A laid-off miner's boy, he takes what he can get, and he's happy to get it!"

She trooped toward the house. Suddenly she noticed the daisies, pansies, and marigolds drooping beside the walk.

"My flowers!" she shrieked. "What's happened to my . . ."

She spun around. I put a protective arm

around Duffy, but Ma never even glanced at him. Her glare centered only on me. Her bottom lip thrust forward and I heard her teeth click.

"Didn't I warn you what would happen if that dog caused any more trouble?"

"Ma. I'll fix it. I'll replace the flowers, I promise. I'll buy a packet of flower seed. Besides, some of these might live."

"I ought to just send him packing this minute, Terence. I ought to—"

"No!" I yelled. "I'll work on the flower bed, Ma. Let's talk about this later, when you're not so mad."

Ma glowered at me. Then she turned and stomped to the door. She stopped and turned toward me. "No more talk about passing up the scholarship, either. I mean it!"

Conrad Baldwin, wearing a pointed blue birthday hat, peered around the half-open door at me and Duffy. His fat face pulled into a pout.

"I'm thick of dogth," he complained.

"You might like seeing one do tricks," I said.

"I hate twickth." He frowned.

Linda had made an attempt to clean up her house. Still, I hardly could find an empty corner to stow my gear.

"Terry! You're right on time." Linda, her baby hanging over one arm and a wad of paper towels

in her other hand, looked glad to see me. A mob
of little kids swarmed around her.

"You don't look like a clown." A tiny girl in a
lavender dress stared up at me.

"I'm not. I'm an animal trainer."

She wrinkled her nose. "Clowns are better. We
had a clown for my birthday party. Named Ruffles."

"Kids. Let's all find a place on the floor to sit
down," Linda said. "Then I'll introduce our
guests."

"I know *him!*" A boy pointed. "He *sings!* He
singded at the park."

"Well, he does tricks with his dog, too," Linda
said, her face hopeful, but worried. I placed my
props around the living room.

"Boys and girls!" I said. The giggling and talking came to a halt. After all my years in choir, I
knew a thing or two about projecting my voice. I
whispered, "Duffy, go to place," and Duffy
jumped onto his platform.

"Duffy and I thank you for inviting us here
today to celebrate Steffie's birthday with you.
Duffy, are you glad to be here?"

"Woof!" Duffy answered.

"Duffy asked me how old Steffie is today. I told
him, and he wants to count out her age in doggie
language. Duffy?"

"Woof! Woof! Woof! Woof!"

A little boy squirmed away from the others and encircled Duffy with his arms. I couldn't allow that.

"Go back and sit down," I said. The boy looked up at me with a blank stare. He didn't move.

Linda realized no one could be near Duffy because I needed to give him cues. She lifted the boy away from Duffy and deposited him among the other children. "Stay!" she ordered.

I performed a couple of simple tricks with Duffy first. I told the kids Duffy had a little cold, and Duffy sneezed. I put a hat on Duffy and said he was going out for a walk, then signaled him to jump off the platform and walk on his hind legs. The kids squealed.

I was a little more worried about the complicated tricks.

"Duffy heard there was going to be refreshments here today."

"I want refreshments," the little girl in the lavender dress said. She got up, and two others started to follow. Linda had said a group of little kids would be a hard audience, and she was right.

"Sit down!" I ordered. The lavender girl looked at me, startled. She sat down and placed her finger up her nose.

"Now, like I said, the dog is ready for something to eat. But first, he's got to set the table."

Duffy went to the corner and pulled a plastic

plate out of the sack. He trotted to the stool I'd placed nearby and set the plate on it. He returned to the sack, pulled out a big metal spoon with his teeth, and placed it next to the plate.

"Looks like you're ready to eat, Duffy. But haven't you forgotten something?" Duffy placed his paws, one on top of the other, on the stool, and dropped his head.

"He'th thaying his prayerth." Conrad peered at the dog, then at me. If Conrad was impressed, I knew it was going good.

After Duffy's imaginary refreshments, he cleared the table. He brought the plate to me, which wasn't right. "He remembered," I ad-libbed, "that it's my night to do dishes."

I was worried we had too little room, but I held up my old Hula-Hoop. "Over!" I ordered, and Duffy jumped through it perfectly. Then he jumped back the other way.

"Duffy," I said, placing a sack on the ground. "Would you help me get ready for school? I need my sneakers." Duffy nosed through the sack and found my tattered sneakers.

"You know, Duffy cares about the environment and hates to see people litter." I said this as I scattered empty pop cans around the living room. Duffy picked them up one by one in his teeth, and put them in a trash basket. I'd only taught him that trick two days before. The kids clapped each time a can clunked to the bottom of the trash can.

When we were done, Duffy took a nice bow. The kids shrieked and clapped their hands together.

"Terry." Linda grabbed my arm. "Terry, how did you do this in such a short time? It was wonderful! Far better than I expected."

I petted Duffy and slipped him another treat. "He's so easy. All I did was follow the instructions in the book. He picked up everything a lot faster than the book said he would."

Duffy sat down on my foot and gazed up at me.

"He's serious about it," Linda said. "He thinks he has a job. Terry, you could expand this act and do it at rodeos this summer. I mean, if you had time between your trips with the choir." She handed me a twenty-dollar bill. I stared at it.

"I can't take this much, Linda."

She shrugged. "That's what Ruffles the Clown charges."

Twenty dollars! The timing couldn't have been better. If I gave the money to Ma, she might not be so mad about the flowers.

"Come in the kitchen and help me dish up cake," Linda said.

I was licking off the cake knife when the back

door opened and Linda's skeleton-looking husband walked in. I'd never seen him with a huge grin. It made him even homelier.

"Linda!" he called. Linda, wiping chocolate off Conrad's fat cheek, stood up. She looked baffled by the enormous smile.

"The mine, Linda!" Ken Baldwin shook his bony skull. "It's going to reopen. Ten days!"

The mine was going to reopen, and Dad would come home. The mine would reopen, and we could pay off our bills. The mine would reopen, and Ma wouldn't have to scrimp and worry over every dime. With luck, Ma's flowers might even revive.

I couldn't quit grinning. I stopped by Linda's front gate, set down my sack of props, and knelt beside Duffy. "We've earned our first paycheck, boy, and we put on a good show, too." Duffy slanted his head and gave me a lick on the chin. "There's no danger of me losing you now," I told him.

CHAPTER NINE

"What kind of pie should we have, Terence?"

Ma scurried around the kitchen, checking the chicken frying on the stove, stirring ingredients into the potato salad, and squeezing lemons for lemonade. It was the night Dad was coming home.

"Chocolate," I said guiltily, knowing Dad liked lemon best. Ma knew it too, so I was surprised when she began melting squares of chocolate in a saucepan.

I was excited for Dad to meet Duffy. To save on phone bills, we'd been talking to Dad only on Sundays, and that hadn't given me enough time to tell him everything about Duffy. I didn't know whether Ma had mentioned in her letters the times Duffy had been in trouble.

About 6 p.m., Dad walked in the front door, set down his suitcase, sniffed the air, and smiled. I leaped up from the couch and gave him a hug. He smelled like a pine forest.

Ma's upper lip pressed over her lower one, hiding a smile. Dad put his arm around her, rubbed his nose against her forehead, and squeezed her.

Ma looked bashful. "Supper's ready," she said. "Let's sit down before it gets cold."

"Let me wash up," Dad said.

I followed Dad into the bathroom. "You're taller, Terry," he said to my reflection in the mirror. He grabbed my head and rubbed my hair with his knuckles. His chest and shoulders felt like slabs of granite.

"So, is logging really dangerous?" I asked. "Did you see anybody get hurt?"

He brought his fingers to his lips, shook his head, and pointed to the kitchen. "Not in front of your ma," he whispered.

When we were seated at the table, Dad lifted his square chin and blue eyes. He touched two fingers to his forehead, to his stomach, and to each shoulder.

"In the name of the Father, the Son, and the Holy Spirit." His eyes misted. I didn't dare look at Ma. I knew she would be staring at her lap, tears rolling.

"Thank you that the mine is open. And that we are together again," Dad said. His mouth twitched a bit. I knew what was coming. "And please. Make Maggie thin. In the name of the Father, the Son, and the Holy Spirit." He crossed himself, peeking at Ma to see if his joke had helped her recover.

Ma blew her nose and pretended to scowl at him. I dished myself some potato salad.

"When do you want to meet Duffy?" I asked.

"What's wrong with now?"

I dashed outside and loosed Duffy, and the dog and I raced to the house. Duffy rushed to Dad, sniffed his jeans, ran to Ma for a quick pat, stopped by my chair, then ran back to Dad.

"Hey, guy, you *are* handsome," Dad said. "Are you as brilliant as Terry says?" Duffy, suddenly quiet, placed his head on Dad's knee and gazed up at him with earnest red-brown eyes.

"This dog looks like one Skinny Wingate, the sheep rancher, used to have."

I tensed.

"I mean, years ago," Dad said. "Wingate's a modest guy, but man, you should have heard him brag on that dog. One day Kelvin Loosli said to him, 'Wingate, is it true, come this fall, that that border collie of yours will be teaching school at Silverbow High?' Ole Wingate, he turned red and answered, 'You're just put out I don't hang around with you anymore. Since I got that dog, I'm used to intelligent company.' "

Mom beamed at Dad.

"Wait till you see Duffy's tricks, Dad," I said.

"I've been hearin' about them." He and Ma exchanged a look. "After supper, how about a demonstration? And tomorrow, let's go fishing up on Wolf Creek. We'll stop at Wingate's on the way back and show him this dog. He'd be crazy about him."

Next morning, Duffy rode between us to Wolf Creek, searching first one side of the road, then the other.

"He looks smart, you know?" Dad said. "When you look into those eyes, something real intelligent looks back at you."

But we'd only been fishing a few minutes when I heard Dad yell, "Hey! Cut that out!" I looked up and saw Duffy was in trouble already. He was gobbling up the first trout Dad had caught.

"Get out of here!" Dad hollered, and Duffy slunk away behind a cottonwood tree. He peered out, his black eye patch exposed, a mournful look on his face.

"He really wants to please," I told Dad. "He won't do it again."

"If he does, we'll leave him at home next time," Dad said. But Duffy understood his scolding, and didn't try to eat any more fish. Every time Dad or I got a fish on the line, Duffy would run back and forth on the creek bank, tail waving, ears perked. When we'd landed the fish on the bank, Duffy would sniff it, wag his tail, then race around in a circle. Almost like he understood a big trout was something to celebrate.

"Wingate used to say his border collie rounded up fish for him," Dad said. "He may have been pulling our legs, but he claimed his dog would wade upstream and flush the fish out of the deep holes. And Skinny would hook them as they swam by."

I knew Skinny and Roma Wingate from church, but not very well. Mrs. Wingate often dabbed at her eyes during Mass. "It's a shame," Ma told me once. "Roma and Skinny have had their disappointments."

We took a rutted road off the highway and wound down to the Wingates' small white farmhouse. Roma Wingate, a round woman with a gray bun on top of her head, was sitting on the front porch shelling peas. In her lap she held a huge metal bowl, a small plastic one, and a yellow cat draped across her knee.

She reached her hand over the porch railing.

"John Riley. Excuse me if I don't get up. Suzette will be upset if I dump her off." She looked at me. "How are you, young man? You sure did sing good on the Fourth of July."

A black-and-white dog, with gray hairs on its muzzle and a coating of film over its eyes, limped onto the porch.

"This is Skinny's old dog, Betsy. Come here to Roma, girl. There, you sit down here." The dog lowered its hind end slowly. "She's almost blind,"

Mrs. Wingate said, "and she can't go out with Skinny and the other dogs anymore. It kills her to stay home. Betsy! Don't you curl your lip at that cat." Roma looked up at me, her eyes bypassing the glasses on her nose.

"She knows she's not supposed to growl at my kitties. All the animals here are my babies, and I tell them they have to get along together, and they understand." She tipped her head. "Dogs and cats are so much smarter than people," she confided.

"John," she said to Dad. "Skinny's up on Cougar Ridge, showing a new herder around." Suddenly Roma Wingate slapped her hand against her chest. "My land, who is that?" I followed her eyes to our pickup truck. Duffy, ears perked, was gazing out the window, eyes pleading.

"That's Terry's new dog," Dad said. "I want to show him to Skinny."

"You'll give him heart failure! He looks so much like Cody, Skinny's best dog. Cody died seven years ago, and Skinny misses him still."

On Cougar Ridge, Dad parked the truck beside a weathered sheep wagon.

"Those are Wingate's sheep," Dad said. We could see, in the distance, white wisps of wool on the hillside. "And there's Skinny." A tall man on a gray horse waved and came loping toward us.

"Let's walk out to meet him," Dad said.

The sun was blazing, but a juniper-fragrant breeze cooled the ridge. Duffy dashed after a butterfly, chased a chipmunk, and, when Skinny Wingate got close enough, ran to greet him.

"I thought my eyes were playin' tricks on me," Skinny said as he swung off his horse. "I thought this dog was my Cody."

"He's a stray Terry found."

Wingate wiped his forehead. "A dead ringer."

Behind Wingate, on the slope, the herder whistled, and two dogs ran toward the sheep. One after another, sheep poked their hind ends into the air to stand, then began to move forward.

"Would we be in the way if we watched the dogs?" Dad asked. Dad's grandpa had come to the Rockies from Ireland to work as a herder, and Dad loved watching sheep and dogs.

"Will your dog stay with you? I wouldn't want 'im to get in and scatter the sheep," Wingate said.

"He'll stay with me," I said. "He knows 'stay' and he minds good."

"I'll walk back up there with you," Wingate said.

At the top of the rise, Wingate jabbed his thumb toward the flock. "This here is a new herder, just come from Peru. I might need to help 'im take the sheep to the creek to water 'em."

Dad pointed. "Look at those dogs move the sheep, Terry." He turned to Skinny. "One summer I stayed with my grandpa in the sheep camp for a couple of weeks. I was pretty young, but I remember the dogs. Grandpa served them each a bowl of oatmeal every morning, just like he made for us."

Wingate wasn't listening. He was shielding his eyes from the sun and watching the herder and the sheep when a black-and-white blur dashed through the rabbit brush and streaked up the hillside.

"Duffy!" I screamed. "No! *Duffy!*"

I hadn't noticed he had left my side. I knew he heard me calling. But he didn't slow down.

"Terry." Dad frowned. "You said he'd . . ."

I leaped over the brush and ran to the adjoining hillside.

"Duffy!" I hollered. I knew Wingate would be mad if Duffy scattered his sheep.

The other dogs, a brown-and-white dog and one too far away for me to see its color, both stopped. They perked their ears at the approaching streak. The herder whistled, and the dogs resumed their work.

Duffy now was within twenty feet of the sheep. If he ran into the middle of them, I worried some might leap off the near cliff, or pile up on top of each other, or die of fright.

Abruptly, Duffy stopped. He dropped to his stomach. He stared at the sheep. Sheep looked over at him nervously. Duffy began to circle, belly low to the ground.

"Duffy! Come!" I yelled.

Duffy ran a few steps toward three sheep that weren't moving down the hill with the others. Two, eyeing the dog, trotted off to join the flock, but one large ewe bolted back toward the meadow. Duffy zipped across a lava outcrop, turned in front of the ewe, and leaped at her head. The ewe jumped into the air with all four feet, then backed up and eyed the dog. After a moment, she turned and ran after the others.

"Duffy!" I screamed.

"It's okay," a voice above me said. I looked up at the towering Wingate. He was staring at the moving mob of sheep. "That dog's good help," he said. "He's some fine dog."

"He knows better! When he comes back . . ." I hissed through clenched teeth.

Wingate pulled his gaze away from the sheep and looked at me.

"He usually minds good!" I said.

"He's mindin' now," Wingate said.

I scowled. "He's not paying *any* attention to me." My voice was loud, even though Wingate stood close.

"Could be he's mindin' somethin' inside 'imself."

"What?" I sounded annoyed.

"Hundreds of years of instinct. Border collies are bred to herd sheep. There's a voice inside 'im he hears louder 'n he hears you."

"He should have minded me," I grumbled.

Duffy followed the sheep to the creek, then ran across the slope toward us. When he came near, he slowed and started walking sideways. At least he knew he'd done wrong.

I stepped forward to lay hold of him. But Wingate stepped in front of me, maybe accidentally. He reached down and touched Duffy's nose with one finger. Duffy searched Wingate's face with sober red-brown eyes.

"You're right about this here dog, John," Wingate said to my dad. "He's quite a bit like Cody."

In late afternoon, Dad and I stopped at Beckman Creek to fish. But the spark had gone out of the day. I hardly talked at all. I'd wanted to impress Dad with my new dog. But once again, Duffy had behaved, as Vic DeFazio said before, "weird."

CHAPTER TEN

I flung open the church's basement door, arranged my face so I'd look unhurried, and walked to my row.

Father Egan was stalking the room. Boys' heads hung like pods on a vine. Mrs. North bit her lip and kept watch on Father with round, troubled eyes. No one even noticed I was late.

I caught Vic's eye. He shook his head and looked down. I elbowed Brad Anderson, the Protestant kid from Redbud. He looked over and frowned. "Shut up!" he hissed.

"I didn't say anything!" I elbowed again. "What's goin' on?" Anderson only narrowed his eyes and glared at me.

Father Egan yanked on his thin hair, lifted his face, and moaned through clenched teeth, "Mr. Finlayson, you might have waited until after my jubilee celebration."

Derek Finlayson, head drooping, shrugged.

"Or given me some warning," Father continued.

Finlayson flung blond hair off his forehead.

"It just happened," he said. "I woke up Saturday morning and . . ." He didn't finish. But his voice told what the problem was. The pitch of his words jumped from low to high. Derek Finlayson, one of our most important singers, had been hit by adolescence and had lost his choir voice.

"We need you so much in the Handel number!" Father Egan shoved his hands into his pockets, paced to the end of the room, and reached up and wrung strands of hair. He stared at the music stand.

"Well, it can't be helped," he said sadly. "Shall we begin?"

Father never really got into the practice, didn't jump around or balance on his toes or anything. When the voice of one of his important singers changed, Father Egan took it hard. If a voice deepened gradually, it gave Father time to get used to the idea. But he was really put out when a voice changed overnight, and every now and then that happened.

When we were passing our music to the end of the row, Brad Anderson mumbled, "Gol', I hope that doesn't happen to me."

"Why not?"

" 'Cause."

"There's lots of other stuff to do besides choir!" I snapped.

"Yeah? What?" Anderson asked. I looked at his face. It was pale and worried.

"You ever heard of fishing?" I asked. "Playing ball? Taking a hike? Watching TV? Riding a bike? Reading a book? Man, if I didn't have to be in choir . . ."

Mrs. Anderson, who'd been sitting in a folding chair waiting for rehearsal to be over, motioned for Brad to come on. As she passed Father Egan she patted him on the arm, like a mourner at a funeral.

On the way home, I asked Vic, "How old is Finlayson?"

"Fourteen. Just turned fourteen."

"Father shouldn't have been surprised, then."

"He's never ready to lose the best singers. He's probably lighting candles that *your* voice won't change until you're eighteen."

I grabbed Vic by the elbow. "Vic, if my voice doesn't change until I'm fourteen, I have two *more* years in the choir."

"Yeah?"

"Do you know when I started choir?"

"Same year as me. When we were nine."

"That's a lot of years of my life! What if I want to do other things?"

"Like?"

"Oh no! You too? Anderson couldn't think of *anything* else a kid could do besides choir."

"This is Silverbow, man. There's not much to do."

"If *I* weren't in choir, I'd do something else."

"What?"

"Duffy and I would appear at every rodeo in the area during the summer. In winter, we'd give demonstrations at schools. We'd entertain at the old folks' home. I'd fill up my calendar with performances for us."

"You'd get tired of it. Just like you're getting tired of choir."

"No. Because it would be something *I* wanted, not something my mom . . ."

I stopped walking. Because the truth of what I was saying hit me. Just like Anderson, I was in choir because my mom wanted me to be. Not that I hadn't enjoyed it at one time. I had. But I didn't anymore. And it was time to speak up and say so. Now that there was something I wanted to do more.

Ma was ironing the sleeve of a wine red choir robe when I walked in. Sweat beaded on her forehead. Her arms, bare in a sleeveless shirt, glistened.

"Terence Michael. How was your day?" she asked.

"Do you sometimes get sick of pressing choir robes?" I asked.

"I'm choir mother, aren't I? It goes with the job."

"I mean, you've been doing it a lot of years."

"Somebody has to." She set the iron on its base and looked up. She wiped her forehead. Then she looked at me with affection. "It's nice of you to worry about me, Terence."

I grabbed crackers from a box on top of the refrigerator and sat down at the kitchen table. I'd have to try another approach.

"How are we doing on money, Ma?"

She beamed. "Your dad's first paycheck from the mine comes home Friday."

"But we're behind, right?"

Ma looked at me, a vertical line starting above one brow.

"Sure. But thank God, we can begin to catch up on our bills now."

"We could use more money, though. Like, if I helped out?"

No tender look came my way now. Ma was beginning to smell a rat.

"You already have a job, with Mrs. Empey. That takes care of Duffy's food and spending money for you. That's enough help. You're only twelve." She picked up the iron and pressed it down on the robe's magenta collar. Steam floated up past her face. "What are you scheming, Terence?"

"Well, I think Duffy and I could get jobs doing a great dog act. If I had more time."

"You don't have time."

"I would . . ." I eased out of the chair and moved over by the sink, in case she threw the iron.

". . . if I quit choir."

"*Quit* choir?" Her eyes flew open, then narrowed to slits. "I knew when I said yes to that dog it was a mistake. Terence, you can't *quit* choir. You're Father Egan's number one soloist."

I didn't know what to say to that.

"And, you're sure to get the choir scholarship."

"I've told you! That's for someone who wants to study music. Dad is working again. I can go to college without the scholarship."

A thunderhead rolled in over Ma's face. "The mine could close again in a year or two! You can't depend on a silver-mining job."

Her expression began to change from anger to panic. "How could you think of leaving the choir with Father Egan's jubilee only a week away?"

"I didn't mean I'd quit before then. I'd quit after. Then I could have the rest of the summer to—"

"Terence!" Ma's chin jutted forward. "In the choir, you are *someone*. You are soloist in a choir that's famous all over the state. And Montana, too."

I thumped my chest.

"I'm someone anyway! Terry Riley! A guy who

loves to work with his dog. And wants more time to do it."

Ma thudded over and looked at me, a tear gleaming on her cheek. She clasped her hands and shook them in my face.

"Terence. It's only for two years."

I started to say something, but she caught hold of my wrist.

"Terence, let's not talk of this anymore, until after the jubilee." She dropped her voice. "You've been doing without for a long time. Maybe the trouble is you want more money. On Friday night, I'll buy you a pair of new sneakers. And you'll see things in a different light, huh?"

She looked so hopeful, I wished I could promise. But I couldn't. I shook my head.

"After Father Egan's jubilee, Ma, I'm quitting choir."

CHAPTER ELEVEN

"Mr. Lenz?" I asked into the telephone.

"You got him. Who's this?"

"This is Terry Riley. Are you head of the Silverbow Stampede?"

"I am. Why?"

"I . . . um, well, I was wondering if you might need a dog act for intermission at the rodeo?"

"Your dog?"

"Uh-huh."

"Well, listen, son, we host a real first-rate rodeo here. Lot of name cowboys come in for it. So if your dog just does a few tricks—"

"No! He does a whole act."

"Could it fill twenty minutes?"

"Yeah! I timed it the other night at fifteen minutes. I could add a couple of tricks, and put in a few more jokes."

"Tell you what. I'll be out at the fairgrounds on Monday morning. Come out and show me your routine. I don't have an intermission act yet—I was going to do some calling around this weekend."

"Thanks! I'll be there."

I pushed the baby buggy onto the sidewalk.

"Up, Duffy!" Duffy placed his paws on the buggy's metal bar.

"Walk, Duffy!" I said, and Duffy, his tail end swaying, began to push the buggy down the street. I grinned. If I dressed Duffy in a frilly hat and apron and came up with a story about Duffy being a mother's helper, I had a new trick for my dog act.

"Okay, Duffy, that's enough." Duffy let go of the buggy and came to me. "Good dog." He snuggled against my leg and peered up with solemn red-brown eyes.

"You sure are smart." I stroked his black-and-white head. The trick book had said it would take a week to teach a dog how to push the buggy. Duffy seemed to have it perfect, and I'd worked with him only one morning.

If I could land the job with Mr. Lenz, Duffy and I would perform before a big crowd. That would get my name out, and bring more jobs our way.

The sun blazed directly overhead. I needed to get inside and take a shower. Father Egan's jubilee celebration would start in late afternoon.

"Duffy, come." I linked Duffy to his chain,

wrapped the chain around our silver poplar, and fastened it. Duffy watched me, a mournful look on his face.

I knelt down and hugged him around the neck. He bathed my neck with his tongue. I looked into his wise eyes.

"I'm going to be gone a long time today, boy. Don't get into trouble. Ma probably wants an excuse to get rid of you. She blames you for me wanting to leave choir. So whatever you do, be good. Don't tangle yourself around the tree, don't chew on the trunk, don't dig a hole in the grass." I looked over at Ma's flowers. Some had lived, and I'd planted new ones, too. Duffy was tied far enough away he couldn't possibly stretch and reach them.

Duffy's eyes searched my face. When he looked at me like that, I had a hard time swallowing.

As I reached the porch, I heard Dad's voice in the kitchen, low and angry.

"Maggie, it's not like he's asking to do something *wrong*."

"It *is* wrong. It's wrong to throw away a chance for a better life." I could tell Ma was crying. "You want him to end up like us?"

"What's so bad about us?"

"What's bad about never knowing from one month to the next if you'll have a job? What's bad about cave-ins and gas pockets and funerals for

miners?" Ma was sobbing now. "I only want—"
She stopped. I think she heard the porch creak.

I walked in like I hadn't heard a thing. Ma was
wiping her eyes on her shirt. Dad put a phony
smile on his face. "Hi, Terry," he said.

"Don't touch those!" Ma slapped my fingers
away from the fancy sandwiches she was taking
to the church. Ma had been cooking and making
things for days. And starving herself at the same
time, so she could get into her peach flowered
dress for Father's jubilee.

"Did you polish your boots, Terence?"

"Yeah."

"You're going for a haircut?"

"Yes, Ma."

"What else?" She screwed up her forehead and
thought. "I guess that's all." She tried to smile,
but her face sagged. She hadn't been able to look
cheerful since I'd told her I planned to quit choir.
She was hoping Father's jubilee would change
my mind, but was scared it wouldn't.

"It's a special day, huh?" she asked. "For Father, for you, for all of us?" She lifted her brows
and tilted her head.

I nodded. Her face looked so wistful, I forced
my mouth up at the corners.

Through the murky barbershop window, I saw
Father Egan in Don Osburn's single barber's

chair. I wanted to leave and come back later, but Father Egan looked out, saw me, and waved his black arm.

I wanted to avoid him. I felt like I had a mortal sin on my soul, not telling him I planned to quit choir, though I knew it would have been mean to upset him before his jubilee.

"Terence!" he called as I walked in. "How's my soloist?" He fluttered his hand in midair. "If you've got a sore throat or a cough, don't tell me. If you've got a fever, I don't want to know. Just tell me you're fine. If it's a lie, I'll absolve you later." He swiveled his head and grinned at Don the barber.

Don nodded and tried to smile, but I saw the muscles in his forearm tighten. Father Egan must have been a tough customer for him, because Father's head was never still.

"Have you heard this guy sing?" Father asked Don, flashing his uneven, yellow teeth at me. Don shook his head. He didn't go to any church—told me once he didn't believe in God.

"You weren't at the Fourth of July program?" Father cranked his head around, sounding amazed. Don tried to follow Father's head with his scissors.

"I went fishing on the Clearwater," Don said. "In two hours I cau—"

"Well, if you haven't heard Terence, you have a treat in store."

I looked away and pretended to study a jar filled with combs in blue liquid.

"You are coming up to the church, aren't you, Don?" Father Egan tossed his head, almost catching a scissors blade in his eye.

"I wasn't planning to."

Don poured some jelly-looking stuff into the palm of his hand. Its sharp smell bit the inside of my nose. Don tried to smear it onto Father Egan's sparse hair, but Father had turned to face him again.

"But *everyone* in town is coming. Lotta people from out of town, too."

Don pressed his hand onto Father Egan's head to hold it in place. With his other hand, he reached for electric clippers and turned them on. He began to shave Father's neck.

"YOU DON'T HAVE TO BE CATHOLIC, DON," he called above the noise of the razor. "AND THERE WILL BE LOADS OF FOOD. YOU SHOULDN'T MISS A CHANCE TO HEAR THE CHOIR. AND TERENCE."

Don whisked hairs off Father's shoulders with a hand broom. Father Egan stood, stretched, and brushed off his black coat. Sweat glistened on his cheeks and brow. The shop's back door stood open, but not a whiff of breeze moved through the shop.

Father Egan paid Don, then came over as I settled into the barber's chair.

"Today, Terence," he said, "don't worry about a thing."

"Okay." I was a little nervous about the big crowd, but I wasn't scared.

"We've practiced hard. Don't worry about the mechanics of singing today. Your voice inflection, where you'll place your feet, that sort of thing." I wasn't worried about where to place my feet.

"Just sing from the heart, Terence." He stood in front of the barber's chair, gripped its arms, and looked me in the eyes. "Your solo, the 'Ave Maria,' will be the highlight. A year, two years from now, people still will be talking about Father Francis Egan's fiftieth anniversary of his ordination to the priesthood, and the soloist of Our Lady of the Snows Boys Choir."

Father Egan's voice, so full of breath and emotion, made me quiver.

If I'd known then how true his words would turn out to be, I would have quivered more.

CHAPTER TWELVE

With the other kids in the choir, I waited at the back of the church.

"Geez, it's hot," Brad Anderson said.

"It's not that bad," I insisted, though trickles of sweat ran down my sides under my choir robe. The thing about Anderson, he was uneasy at Catholic services. Afraid he'd do something wrong, like stand when he should kneel, kneel when he should sit. And today, because everything was so elaborate, he was real jittery and getting on my nerves. I could get nervous myself looking at the packed church.

Ushers had propped open the church's tall front doors plus a side door at the front of the sanctuary. But the August air from outdoors did nothing to make it more comfortable. Normally the church's high ceilings kept the sanctuary cool, but the crowd had heated up the place. Ushers already were bringing in folding chairs for the overflow crowd.

Julia North, looking like nobody I'd ever seen, bustled in with her music. She wore a green dress and her hair looked plastered to her head. She

sat down at the organ, squinted across the church
to find Father Egan in line with the other priests,
then, at a signal, depressed the organ pedals with
all her might.

Altar boys started down the center and side
aisles wearing red robes, waist-length white sur-
plices, and white gloves. Four in front, including
Vic DeFazio's little brother Tim, carried fat,
lighted candles. I turned around and tried to get
Vic's attention, but he was busy watching Tim.

Behind the candle bearers walked two boys
with wooden crosses. Next came Paul Randall, a
lanky ranch kid with oily blond hair, shaking a bit
with his gold crucifix. His white gloves gripping
the wooden base had dark stains, like tractor
grease, on them. I finally caught Vic's eye, flicked
my head toward the procession, and grinned.

Altar boys followed, carrying banners with cut-
outs of butterflies and doves and words like *Peace*
and *Love*.

Our choir began to move down the center aisle,
singing *"This is the day, this is the day that the Lord
has made . . ."* I glanced from side to side. Mr.
Broman, the grocer, sat near the back, his arm
draped over the edge of the pew. He looked different. The paper clip on his glasses was
gone—he had brand-new frames. I guess he was
more prosperous with the mine open and people

paying off their charge accounts. (I'd paid off my hot dogs weeks before.)

There were people in the pews I didn't recognize. They'd driven over from nearby towns. Others I knew from town, but I'd never seen them in church before.

"You want a new dress?" Dad had asked my mom. Ma, always thrifty, had said, "No." That afternoon she hadn't managed to squeeze into her peach flowered dress either. So she'd brightened up her tired gray dress with a turquoise scarf, and curled her hair fancy.

When she saw me, her eyes misted. Dad's, too. I tried to remember that Ma would have been weepy even if I hadn't said I was quitting choir.

I passed Skinny and Roma Wingate, and they smiled. Then, from the front pew, a pudgy face scowled up at me. I grinned down at Conrad Baldwin. His mother tugged on him to get back in his place. Linda didn't go to any church—she and Conrad had come just to hear me sing.

We filed into pews near the altar. Behind us marched priests in black cassocks, with embroidered stoles in bright colors over their shoulders. I glanced at Vic. Vic nodded toward Father Tony, the priest from Redfish who said masses at Our Lady of the Snows when Father Egan was out of town on choir trips. A young guy with coal black hair, Father Tony, was passing in front of me. His fingers were pressed together in a steeple.

Father Egan, wearing a green robe with silver braid that all but covered his black cassock, walked with a reverent, solemn gait. But his eyes darted about, taking in the packed pews, the fancy clothes, the enthralled faces.

Bishop Fremont, a short man with round glasses, followed the priests. He carried a large wooden staff and wore a tall funny hat that ended in a point. Unlike nearly everyone else, the bishop wasn't wearing a grave expression. His eyes, roaming the pews, twinkled.

A priest stood at the front of the church and swung a brass incense censer. A heavy fragrance like burning leaves invaded the choir pews, and my head felt woozy. Suddenly the importance of the occasion and the number of people present struck me. I had a moment of panic. What if the heat and incense made me faint?

Father Tony led the opening prayer. Another priest walked to the lectern to read the Scripture. When I sat down, my confidence returned. After all, I'd never fainted at a choir appearance before.

I fidgeted with my collar, blew hair off my forehead, and only pretended to mouth the words to the prayers. My solo, the "Ave," would come before the bishop gave the sermon.

Then Anderson nudged me. "Hey, you're on!"

I rose from the pew, hoping I looked calm. A beam of sunlight poured through the stained-glass window behind me and fell across the side of my face, onto my music.

Mrs. North began to play the beautiful first measures. I thought the "Ave" probably was the prettiest song ever written, and with all my heart I wanted to do it well. I sucked in a huge breath.

"Aaaaaaa-ve Ma-reeeee-a," I began. *"Maaaaay-den mild."* I was in good voice.

"Ah! Lis-ten to your child's prayer . . ." Sometimes I could hear, in my voice, the quality of purity people talked about. Today was one of those times.

"For Thou canst hear amid the wild . . ." I lifted my chin and sang to the ceiling beams. In the fifth row, my brawny dad brushed away a tear.

" 'Tis Thou, 'tis Thou canst save amiiiiiid . . . de-spair." The organ, the notes, the words flowed together, coming not from Mrs. North and me, but through us, like sunlight streaming through the stained-glass windows.

"We slumber safely 'til the morrow . . ." Linda Baldwin, I noticed, dabbed her eyes. I breathed in, and when I exhaled, more music escaped.

"Though even by men outcast, reviled." I glanced at Father Egan. He was looking past me, above the altar, to where the sunlight broke into colors. My voice caught a moment. It didn't sound like an error; it added emotion.

"Oh, Maiden, see a maiden's sorrow; Oh, Mother, hear a suppliant child!" I noticed a shadow at the side door.

"Aaaaa-ve Ma-reee-a." Something like a fist jabbed my stomach. The shadow was black and white.

"Unnnnnn-defiled." Duffy, trailing a broken chain, crept across the church's tile floor. The broken chain went scritchascritchascritch.

I'll pretend he's not here, I thought. He must have twisted the chain until one of its links busted. But if I keep a grip on myself, Duffy coming in here won't ruin anything.

"The flinty couch whereon we're sleeping . . ." The dog padded up the carpeted stairs. The bishop's odd-shaped hat listed to one side. He was leaning over, trying to see if his eyes were playing a trick. Duffy trotted over and sat down by the railing in front of me.

"Shall seem with down of eider piled . . ." A wooden tone began to creep into my voice.

"If Thou above sweet watch art keeping."

Somewhere, nearby, a siren started. I gulped air, determined to drown it out.

"The murky cavern's air so heavy . . ."

I looked down at Duffy, seated beside the rail, and gasped with horror. The siren I'd heard was him. Head thrown back, he was howling!

"Shall breathe of balm . . ."

Titters began to run through the pews. I heard a little kid say, "Hear de doggie?"

". . . if Thou hast smiled." My voice sounded full of desperation. I didn't dare look Father Egan's way.

"Oh, Maiden . . ."

"AAAAAOOOOOOOOOOOOOO!" sang Duffy.

A mother in a front pew, trying not to smile, clamped her hand over a small girl's mouth. The girl was stabbing the air with her finger.

"Oh, Maiden, hear your child pleading . . ." My notes were wobbling. I didn't know if I could go on.

"AAAAAAOOOOOOO," Duffy moaned.

The dog trainer in Linda couldn't stand it. She rose, pushed Conrad back onto the pew, and came up the center aisle.

"Oh, Mother, hear a suppliant child!" I sang.

Trying to be inconspicuous, Linda slipped up the stairs, took hold of Duffy's leash, spoke a harsh "Come!" under her breath, and stole down the stairs and out the side door.

The organ continued to play. My mouth was open, but nothing came out. Anderson nudged me. I gripped his wrist and wrenched it hard. He gasped and shrunk back, and I slipped past him.

I ran down the stairs, looking straight at the gray carpet, then fled out the side door. The notes of the "Ave" chased after me.

Linda was a half block away, under an elm tree, scolding Duffy.

I couldn't look at her. Molten shame burned in me, and I couldn't speak. Without even telling her thank you for helping, I snatched Duffy's leash and dragged him up the sidewalk.

"Terry!" Linda called after me. "Where are you going?"

CHAPTER THIRTEEN

I dragged Duffy up the hill, my choir robe winding around my knees. I yanked him through the alley, all the way to my house.

"You dummy!" I yelled. "You ruined everything! How could you do it?"

I was scared of what Ma and Dad would do to me, but they wouldn't be home for a while. No matter how disgraced they felt, they would stay for Mass.

"You're looking for a new home," I hissed at Duffy. "Ma and Dad will make me give you away."

I would write Ma a note, telling her I realized Duffy had to go. If she read it in a letter, maybe there wouldn't have to be a huge scene with crying and threats.

I felt sad, humiliated, and mad. Mad at the dog and mad at myself, for not preventing the disaster at the church. Ma and I had made an agreement about Duffy. If he ever caused too much trouble . . . Still, I couldn't stand the thought of parting with him.

I flung off my robe and hung it on the hook beside the kitchen door. I dashed into my bedroom, kicked off my shiny boots, and threw off my dress shirt and pants. I grabbed an old T-shirt out of the laundry basket and pulled on a pair of jeans and my holey tennis shoes, without socks.

Duffy crept into the bedroom and sat down in the corner, eyes on the floor.

"You'd better be sorry," I told him. I'd been feeling tired of choir and indifferent toward Father Egan's celebration, but now I realized how I felt loyal toward the old man, too. I couldn't think about how much disappointment I'd caused him.

I collected paper and a pen from a kitchen drawer. I'd write Father a letter too, resigning from choir. I'd planned that note already, but it was different now. Now Father would accept it gladly.

"C'mon," I ordered Duffy. "Let's go to the hills." I wanted to take a final walk with Duffy and find a private place where I could write my letters. When I came back, I'd leave Duffy off at Linda's so Ma and Dad would never have to see him again.

My shoelaces were dragging when I reached the road that wound up to Mount Columbine. I hadn't even taken time to tie them. I knelt down. Duffy sidled over to me. He reached out his head, eyes pleading, a show of pink tongue sneaking from his mouth. I stood up quickly. If I didn't stay mad at him, it would be too hard.

To the southwest, thunderheads were rolling up behind the peaks. A smell of rain wafted down from the high country. Threads of lightning splintered the sky behind Columbine Peak, and a moment later, the mountain rumbled.

My spirits lifted at the prospect of rain. Dust coated the bunchgrass, sagebrush bushes, and lava outcrops, making everything gray.

I left the road and started to hike up the hillside. Duffy sniffed the air, squinted into the wind, and tucked in his tail. He hung behind.

"C'mon!" I ordered. "You hang around town, someone's apt to shoot you before I can give you away."

Duffy whimpered, something I'd seldom heard him do. A gust of wind struck me in the face then. Duffy didn't like wind, I knew, but an approaching storm just hit my mood.

I hiked toward an aspen grove on the ridge above. My gloominess made me walk fast. Already I'd lost sight of the town below. Duffy still hung back; I had to turn and call him every few minutes.

When rain began to fall, I felt glad. I lifted my head and let drops splash my face. If it rained

and rained and rained, I would get soaked. I
wanted to be even more miserable.

"This is a rotten day!" I shouted to the storm.

Beads of rain struck the ground and made cra-
ters on the brick-dry ground. I placed the yellow
tablet paper inside my shirt so it wouldn't get wet.

Duffy and I reached the aspen grove. But it
didn't offer much shelter because the trees were
too far apart. Rain began to fall in sheets. Duffy
huddled next to me. He moaned. Water ran off
his haunches, darkening his coat to blue-black.
He smelled like wet dog.

Since I was getting wet anyway, I moved out
from the aspens and walked up the mountainside. I remembered a cave on the north face of
Columbine. I decided to swing left and try to find
it. I didn't mind getting wet, but I was beginning
to feel dumb. Any kid who grows up in the mountains should know better than to leave home without a coat. Weather can change drastically, even
on a hot August day.

The hillside was steeper now, and in some
places I had to scramble over rock. When I
reached a deer trail, Duffy suddenly ran in front
of me and almost made me fall.

"Watch out!" I complained.

Duffy, eyes squeezed tight against the rain,
bumped my knees.

"Move!" I scolded, and raised my foot in a threat.

Duffy whined.

"I didn't know you were such a coward," I said. "It's only a little rain." He wouldn't move. "Go on back to town, if you want. Maybe you can get dinner at the church." Thinking about all the food I was missing at the celebration made me mad. I reached down and shoved Duffy out of my way.

He yelped. Like I'd really hurt him. Then he crouched in front of me and blocked my path again.

"Quit it!" I yelled. He scooted up by my feet. I saw he was tugging on my shoelaces.

"Hey!" I yelled. I retied my shoelaces, then I pointed. "Go home, Duffy!"

This walk wasn't the farewell I'd had in mind. Duffy fell in behind me, but his ears were flat against his head. He didn't block the path anymore, but he still hung behind.

Now all I wanted to do was push ahead and find shelter. My letter-writing plan was shot because the paper against my chest was soaked.

I walked a few minutes more, and my head started to settle down. And then a thought hit me. Maybe Duffy was trying to warn me of something. I wondered about bears, but decided a bear wouldn't be out in this rain. I shielded my eyes and looked up the hillside to see if we were within sight of the cave. In that moment, the rain turned to snow.

I swung around to look at Duffy. "Sorry, Duffy," I said. "I should have listened." A mountain snowstorm could be dangerous.

Bless me, Father, for I have sinned. I shoved my dog when he was trying to help me. Swirling snow hid the upper mountain. I didn't know whether we were close to the cave or not. I considered turning around. But if snow was hitting the entire mountain, I'd be no better off. Visibility was worsening by the moment, and I didn't want to end up wandering in circles.

I had a spooky memory suddenly, of two hikers who had been caught in an early snow years before. Dad had helped search for them. One was wearing shorts and neither had a coat. The woman lived, but the man died of hypothermia.

Bless me, Father, for I have sinned. I sneaked off to the park to train Duffy. I charged hot dogs at Broman's. I caused my parents to fight. Duffy was turning white from snow. I leaned over and petted him. "I think the cave is our best bet now." Once at the cave, I could collect branches and start a fire. I remembered then I had no matches. Being cold and soaked suddenly filled me with alarm. I was worried about hypothermia.

If I never get to confession again, Father in Heaven forgive my sins. If we reached the cave, I figured, at least the dog and I would be out of the weather. We could huddle together, maybe pile pine branches on ourselves.

I dropped my head and began to push up the mountain. *Holy Mary, Mother of God, pray for us sinners now and at the hour of our death. Amen.* Judging by how long and how fast I'd walked, I knew the cave couldn't be much farther. But it was hard to see a yard ahead of me. And either the wind had picked up or I was in the grip of fear, because it was hard to breathe.

My hands felt numb. I tried to stick them in my jeans pockets and discovered something that panicked me. I couldn't aim my hands where I wanted them to go. I remembered that losing coordination was a sign of hypothermia.

That was my last sensible thought. I lost interest in finding the cave or in getting home. I just wanted to lie down and get some sleep.

A ways off, I saw a white mound that looked like a pillow. Probably it was a rock coated with snow. It looked so inviting I started to move toward it.

Duffy barked behind me. He moved off the path and blocked my way. I smiled. First he didn't want me on the path, now he didn't want me to leave it. My silly dog couldn't make up his mind.

"Good dog, nice dog," I mumbled. Memory of the ruined celebration had vanished. I reached out to touch my dog, but my arm didn't work.

"I'm sleepy, Duffy. Got to get a little nap. Then we'll go on." I couldn't remember where we were heading to, but it didn't scare me anymore. I stumbled, fell on my hands, and got up again.

Duffy was acting strange. As I stumbled toward the snow pillow, he jumped onto my leg, bared his teeth, and growled. "Nice dog," I said. I hoped I was smiling at him, but it seemed my mouth wasn't working right. My mind tried to grab at why it was important to smile at the dog, but reaching the pillow so I could take a nap pushed other thoughts away.

I didn't remember lying down. I remember trying to tell Duffy thank you, because he was barking a lullaby for me. Barking and barking and barking.

The land stretched out empty and white. Making no noise, an animal moved through gray fog toward me. When it got closer, I saw it was a wolf.

I felt no fear. I tried to lift my head and call to it, but I couldn't break through the silence.

The wolf padded toward me, eyes shining in the mist. I shut out the sight of him. Then, beside my ear, I heard snuffling. A wet muzzle touched my cheek.

I felt scratching on my arm. Then a weight moved onto me, pressing down from my chin to my hips. In the stillness I heard breaths, inhaling and exhaling.

From what seemed a long way off, something broke the quiet. A long, grieving howl.

CHAPTER FOURTEEN

My eyes were closed, but I could see white fields. Someone was pulling on me. I seemed to float.

A low voice broke through the silence. One of my eyes was pried open, and a stranger with a waxed mustache stared into it. He lifted my lip and poked around, and I fell back to sleep.

It seemed I was floating on a warm sea. I opened my eyes. I was in a tub filled with water. A guy in a white smock held me, arm around my shoulders. A woman with a stethoscope was listening to my chest.

"Who are you?" I asked. My voice sounded weird.

"Don't worry, Terry, you'll be okay." She smiled. She spoke to someone behind me. "Dan, go tell Mrs. Riley her son is conscious."

I rested my head on the man's forearm. The ceiling was white, like the mountainside.

"What do you think about his feet?" the man holding me whispered.

"Too soon to know," the woman whispered back. "They don't look good."

After a time two men lifted me onto a stretcher and wheeled me to a room. I must have fallen asleep as soon as they settled me onto the bed.

I heard a woman crying, and I opened my eyes. Ma was leaning over me, nose and eyes swollen. She tucked a blanket up around my chin. Dad said, "Terry?" and squeezed my hand. I heard a faint clicking and recognized it as rosary beads.

I drifted back to sleep. When I awoke, I asked Ma, "Where am I?"

"Thank God," she said. "Terence? Could you take a little bit of broth?" Ma propped pillows behind me and spooned soup into my mouth. "My throat hurts," I complained, and fell back to sleep.

Later, Dad was sitting beside my bed. I reached for him.

"Ah, Terry." He sighed.

"Where am I?"

"You're at the Silverbow Clinic. I sent Maggie home for a nap. She was up all night."

"What happened?"

"A snowstorm moved in on the range."

"Yeah, I remember."

"You took a fall?"

"No. I took a nap."

Dad nodded. "Dr. Lewis said that was a possibility. Sleepiness goes with hypothermia."

"Mr. Riley," a nurse in an orange smock interrupted. "Telephone for you. You can take it at the nurse's desk."

I fell back to sleep again. When I awoke, Dad was sprawled awkwardly over a red chair, snoring.

His muscular chest rose and fell. The room held another bed, neatly made up with white sheets and a blanket. A window with half-closed blinds looked out on a sunny green lawn and a rock garden with orange poppies in it. My throat felt raw.

Dad snorted, and startled himself awake.

"Terry! You're awake? How do you feel?"

I stretched. "So, what happened?"

"First, I've got something to tell you. Maggie called here. Couldn't sleep at home. Wanted you to know, as soon as you woke up, that it's okay about the dog. I mean, forget about what happened at the jubilee. You don't have to give Duffy away."

"No?" The jubilee seemed a hundred years ago. Duffy, too.

"Where is he?"

"At home," Dad declared. He peered from under his thick brows. "Maggie bought him a steak, all for himself. And cooked it, too, in case Duffy doesn't like raw meat. You ever heard of such a thing? And she got a length of heavy chain and a strong hook from the ranch store. I don't think he can get away now."

"Ma wants him to stay?"

"She's scared to death he'll run away to find you and get hit by a car." Dad shook his head and grinned. "That's going to be the most spoiled dog on earth."

I felt bewildered. "She's not mad at him?"

"Mad?" Dad's mouth dropped. Then he shut it. "Well, I guess you don't know, do you? Duffy saved your life."

Ma came to the hospital later. While I ate a bowl of soup, they told me the whole story.

"We came home from Mass, boiling mad. If I'd gotten hold of you then . . ." Ma doubled her fist.

Dad scowled at her. He patted my thigh. "That's water under the bridge. Anyway, I wasn't worried when you weren't home, but your ma was. I figured you'd gone someplace to be alone. I did that a lot when I was a kid, and I told Maggie—"

"And I told *you*, 'Look at those clouds moving in.' I said, 'I hope Terence isn't up on the mountain.' I checked your room, and your coat was in the closet. I got worried about you out in shirtsleeves with a storm moving in."

Dad bounced his hand in front of his chest. "I

told her, 'Terry is a sensible kid. He'll run for shelter if the weather turns bad.' "

Ma glared at Dad. Dad looked sheepish.

Dad asked me, "The storm move in sudden? You didn't have time to get in?"

"I wasn't thinking good. I should have headed back when it started to rain."

Ma raised her chin at Dad and lowered her lashes, like curtains falling.

"We called the Wingates and asked if it was snowing up their way. When Roma said yes, I phoned the search and rescue team."

"You would've felt silly, Ma, if I'd turned up at Vic's house."

"I'd checked there! You sound like your dad. He kept saying 'Now, Mag, no need to panic.' "

"What time did they rescue me?"

"About nine thirty. There was a bit of light still on the mountain. That didn't help them find you, but it helped them get you down."

Dad said, "You were behind a row of boulders. They could have walked within two feet of you and never seen you. Dr. Lewis said as low as your body temperature was, you couldn't have lasted the night."

"How did they find me then?"

"Dr. Lewis said she never heard of such a—" Dad began.

"If it hadn't been for—" Ma said.

"*I'll* tell it, Mag," Dad said.

"Skinny Wingate and two other ranchers were scouring the face of Mount Columbine. Another team was hunting for you on the back of the mountain. Other volunteers were checking out Mount Caribou.

"The wind was making a terrible racket. But Skinny thought he heard barking and howling. The other two figured it was coyotes, but Wingate remembered meeting Duffy, and how smart he was."

Dad scooted his chair closer. "Skinny walked and walked. All of a sudden, out of the blinding storm, jumped Duffy. The dog must have heard or sensed Wingate. He led Skinny right to where you were lying.

"Skinny said your clothes were frozen stiff, except on your chest and torso. They were warm to his touch. Duffy climbed up on your chest and lay there while Skinny waited for the others to arrive with the sled and blankets. Skinny said the dog must have lain on you the whole time, keeping you warm. Duffy even rode down the mountain on your chest."

When Ma spoke, her chin quivered. "Dr. Lewis said Duffy's body heat made the difference. And of course, if Duffy hadn't kept barking . . ." She flicked away tears. "When I think of that dog, lying on top of you in the snowstorm, barking and barking . . ."

Dad patted Ma's leg. He blew his own nose. A shiver ran through me. I'd known Duffy was really smart, but I'd never expected to hear a story like that.

Finally I asked, "How come my throat is so sore?"

"Soon as they got you here, they inserted a tube down your throat to put warm fluids into your stomach. To help bring up your temperature."

Suddenly I remembered something.

"Ma, are my feet . . ."

Ma shot Dad a quick look. "Hush, Terence. Don't think about that now. They don't know yet how bad the frostbite is."

I nodded, my chest tightening with panic. My feet burned like crazy, even though the nurse had given me a pill for pain. I remembered a movie I'd seen about a guy in Alaska who'd frostbitten his feet so bad they had to be amputated.

CHAPTER FIFTEEN

Midmorning next day, I heard a squeaking outside my hospital room. Roma Wingate, pushing a cart with paper cups on it, rolled into view.

"I'll tell Skinny you don't look so bad," she called. "What kind of juice you want, orange or grape?"

"Grape," I said. "Are you a volunteer here?" Roma nodded, and picked up two cups.

"Here. Have one of both. Your mama told me they're trying to push fluids down you."

Fists on her hips, she watched me guzzle the juices.

"My land, Terry, you ought to hear that Skinny Wingate take on about that dog of yours. The lamb buyer come by yesterday, and ole Skinny bent his ear for an hour telling about the rescue.

"You know, when they got you here to the clinic, the dog tried to sneak in. He sat by the emergency room door and moaned his head off. Skinny had to carry him out and put him in the cab of his truck."

"Tell Skinny thanks for me."

"Come out to the place when you get better, and tell him yourself."

After Roma left, I stared at the ceiling plaster. I found two horses prancing on ocean waves. I was beginning to feel like I was back in my own body again, but my swollen, discolored toes throbbed. Duffy and I could come up with a great dog act now and schedule lots of performances. But for that, wouldn't I need my feet?

Old Nellie Empey came to visit, and brought me a warm cinnamon roll.

"Now, Terry, your mama told me your throat was awful sore, too sore to eat. So I put plenty of icing on this roll so it would just slide down. Hee-HEE, heeHEE. Eat up now. I need my hired man back. Your dad come over and did my grass this morning, before he left for work." She wagged her finger. "He won't take a nickel for it. You hurry out of here."

I don't know if it was my imagination, but I thought she glanced toward my feet.

I was eating lunch when I heard someone hiss, "Hey!" Vic DeFazio tiptoed into my room.

"They wouldn't let me in," he whispered. "Because I'm not an adult. So I sneaked up the back stairs. Here." He handed me a chocolate bar.

"Thanks." I sat up, dangling my feet over the bed. My toes weren't as purple as the night before, but they looked pretty ugly. Vic stared at them.

"How's choir?" I asked.

"It's okay . . . now. It took Father Egan a while to recover from your dog's solo."

"What happened after I left the church?"

"Father tried to be as serious as he could, like nothing had happened. But the spell was broken. People had a hard time keeping their kids under control."

I shook my head. I didn't know what to say.

"The bishop, he mentioned the dog in his sermon. Kind of made a joke of it. And the choir's last piece went great. We sounded fab-u-lous."

I nodded.

"The food was fantastic! I ate three platefuls. You should've seen Anderson. He ate like a hog, then got sick and puked all over the grass."

I gazed at my big toe, where skin was pulling back from the nail. Vic pretended not to gawk.

"Hey," he said after a while. "You're comin' back to choir, aren't you? When you're better? I don't have anybody to mess around with." I hadn't told Vic about my plans to quit, because I knew he'd try to talk me out of it.

I shrugged.

Vic stayed only a few minutes more, then he snuck off down the hall.

I heard a voice outside call, "Ter-ry!" I looked

out the window. Linda Baldwin, bouncing on her toes, waved. Next to her, his eyes on Linda's face, stood Duffy.

Linda pointed at Duffy and told him *"Walk."* Duffy stood on his hind legs and pranced down the sidewalk. Linda made her arms into a hoop. Duffy sailed through them. Then Linda tried to aim Duffy's head so he would look up at my second-floor window but of course it didn't work. I fumbled with the window, trying to open it, but it was stuck.

I watched Linda and Duffy move off down the street. My head felt squeezed, like a tight hat was pinching it. What if Duffy could *walk*, but I couldn't?

In late afternoon I struggled to the bathroom at the end of the hall. The nurse escorted me down, but I wanted to try walking back by myself.

I winced every time I took a step. But even if my feet hurt, I didn't want to part with them.

Hobbling toward my room, I turned the corner and saw a man in black. It was Father Egan, talking to a nurse, his white hair bobbing against his head, his arms waving. I sucked in my breath and flattened myself against the wall.

Now what would I do? If only I'd been in my room, I could have pretended to be asleep.

The nurse looked up, saw me with my back

plastered to the wall, and said, "Oh, Father. Here he is now."

Father Egan turned, folded his glasses up slowly, and came toward me. If my feet hadn't been so sore, I would have run. I would have done anything to avoid seeing Father face to face.

"Terence." Father's voice was low. He looked into my eyes and squeezed my shoulder. I flinched.

"Want some help?" he asked.

"No. I'm fine."

"Why are you standing here?"

"I'm . . . resting."

"Let me help you back to your room."

Father put his hand under my elbow and we began to move down the hall. Father Egan always darted from place to place, but he pushed along so slowly I could have counted to twenty-five between each step. That was okay with me—I had no reason to want to be alone with Father.

At the door to my room, I stopped. I forced myself to look at him.

"Father." I had to look down. "I'm sorry I ruined your celebration." My voice cracked.

Father's forehead flew into wrinkles. Then it relaxed. "Let's get you to bed, Terence."

I climbed into bed and wound a blanket over my shoulders. Father pulled up a chair and sank into it.

"Terence, for two years I had looked forward to that celebration. And for the past six months, I'd devoted some part of every day to planning for it."

I fiddled with the blanket. It hurt me to hear him.

"Fifty years a priest. Think of that, Terence!" He sprang out of the chair and began to pace. "And what was my biggest achievement in that half century? *Our Lady of the Snows Boys Choir, Terence.*" Father Egan brought his hands down on the tray that held my water. The tray quivered.

"I dreamed of raising up a choir." He lifted his arm and stared at his open palm. "A choir from a small, isolated town, where there was nothing else for boys. A choir that would give the town, and its kids, something to be proud of." He bent over, his face close to mine.

"And I did! Father Francis Egan made a glorious choir for boys and gave a sorry little mining town *pride* in itself! And Terence, your voice makes that choir even grander. I wanted to show everyone, the people in town, people from nearby towns, priests from around the state, and the bishop too how great we really are."

I nodded, mouth ajar. I'd never thought of it exactly like that. Suddenly Father's eyes narrowed.

"What's wrong with this thinking, Terence?"

"Um . . . I don't know."

He cocked his head and hissed the answer. "*Pride! That* was what was wrong with wanting to impress everyone with my choir." He locked his fingers in front of his face. "Terence. It wasn't my choir." His voice climbed. "It was never my choir. It was *God*'s choir."

He grabbed the chair by its back, lifted it, then plunked it down. "Do you know what God does to prideful people, Terence?"

I shook my head.

"Terence." Then, in a whisper, "Terence. He plays a *joke* on them." Father Egan fell into the chair, threw back his head, and slapped his chest. "Ha! Ha! Ha!" he roared.

" *'He has scattered the proud and all their plans.'* That's St. Luke." Father choked. " *'The exalted will be brought low.'* That's Old Testament, somewhere."

My thoughts were a spinning gyroscope. Father wiped his eyes. "Whooo! And how did God pull off his little joke? He enlisted the help of"—he shielded his eyes with his hand—"the help of a . . . Ha! Ha! Ha! . . . dog!"

"So you're not . . . mad?"

He shook his head. "A foolish old man? That I am. Mad? Oh, no." He sobered. "And here's the odd part, Terence. I had hoped my jubilee celebration would be something to remember. And if it had gone flawlessly, people might have remembered it for two, three, even five years. But *now*"—he waved his arms—"twenty years from now, they'll *still* be telling the story of Father Francis Egan's fiftieth anniversary Mass. Ha, ha! Won't they now?" He stabbed me on the arm.

"Yeah. I guess." Some of the worry and guilt began to leave me.

"Ha! There's a smile. Good. Terence, you need to get a kick out of this too. Hadn't been for you . . ." Father chuckled, cleaning his glasses.

Mrs. Whitcomb, the afternoon nurse, peered in. She carried a tray with a blood pressure cuff, a hypodermic needle, and those little white cups with pills in them. She took a step into the room, but Father Egan gave her a warning stare. Mrs. Whitcomb moved on down the hall.

If I waited, I'd lose my courage too. So I spoke right then.

"Father. I plan to quit choir."

Father cocked his head. "But Terence, I'm not mad at you."

"It's not that. I'm . . . tired of choir." I winced, like I expected him to hit me. Father Egan only stared at me.

"Tired? But Terence, don't we have fun? Don't we go places and see things? Don't we sing the most thrilling music ever written?"

"Yeah. It's just . . . there's something I like better."

"What?" He threw out his hands.

"The dog. I have an act I do with him. And if I had more time, I could get lots of jobs performing. I figured I'd be in choir always, until my voice changed, I mean. But this summer, I found the dog and trained him, and I realized, I'm tired of choir."

Father Egan stared at the floor, his shoulders slumped.

"Terence. This is a terrible loss for me. And I can't help but think it's not a smart decision for you. You were almost a shoo-in for the scholarship."

"I want the rest of this summer, and after school this year, and next summer to work with Duffy. He's really smart, Father, and I want to learn everything I can about training him so we can have a really good act."

"What does Maggie say?"

"She hopes I'll change my mind."

Father nodded. He put his glasses on, folding first one earpiece over an ear, then the other. He peered up to where the walls met.

"You're sure it has nothing to do with the episode at the jubilee? You're not worried about the other boys? I could talk to them."

"It's not that. Honest."

"This is unexpected, Terence. It's your choice, after all, but no one like you has ever quit before. The boys who've quit before were troublemakers, or kids whose parents weren't behind them."

"Father." I cleared my throat. "It's a neat choir. It's just not for me."

"Not for you," he muttered, with a bitter laugh. "The clearest, purest voice God ever gave me to work with, and choir's not for you."

He gazed at me. I could see terrible sadness in his eyes.

"Oh my, Terence." He sighed. "I'm old, but life still holds surprises for me."

He lifted his hand, gave me his blessing, and said, "Rest and get better."

He shuffled out, eyes on the polished floor. I wanted to call, "Wait! I'm sorry." I *was* sorry to disappoint Father. But I wasn't sorry for quitting choir. I wanted to do something else more.

I smacked my pillow and lay back into it. Mrs. Whitcomb returned.

"Will Dr. Lewis be by after dinner?"

"She will."

"And will she tell me what's going to happen about my feet?"

"She will," Mrs. Whitcomb answered.

I couldn't read anything in her face about what the verdict would be.

CHAPTER SIXTEEN

Dr. Lewis strode into my room, head down, looking at papers on a clipboard. She wore a jogging suit and high-priced tennis shoes like they advertise on TV.

"Terry, how are you?" she asked.

"Scared, I guess."

She looked up. "Of me?"

"Of what you might say about my feet."

Her eyebrows lifted. "What?"

"If they're bad, don't they . . . cut 'em off?"

"They have to be pretty bad. Especially on a young person."

Dr. Lewis flung back the sheet. She lifted my foot by the heel.

"Hmmm." She set her clipboard down on a chair. With her thumb and forefinger she took hold of my big toe.

"Well?" I asked.

"This little piggy went to market," she whispered. She grinned at me. "Smile, Terry, they're going to be all right. Ugly for a while, but fine. When they first brought you in, I was worried we might lose you. Then I worried about your feet. Holey, wet sneakers aren't very good footwear for hiking in snow. But the circulation in your toes is okay. You won't run too fast for a while, and these toes will hurt for many years whenever it gets cold."

She patted my foot and lowered it to the bed. "You're a lucky kid. Lucky they found you in time."

"Where's Duffy?" I asked as Dad helped me in the car to go home. "Why didn't you bring him along?"

"You'll see him soon enough," Dad said. "Hey, a Mr. Lenz with the Silverbow Stampede called. He read about you and Duffy in the paper. He booked another act for this year's rodeo, but he wants to meet you and Duffy when you're feeling better."

At the house, I walked barefoot to the door, slower than usual, but as fast as I could. I threw open the screen and started to call Duffy.

"Terence," Ma said. She held Duffy in a sitting position on a kitchen chair. Duffy, wearing a party hat, a bow on his collar, and one of Ma's scarves around his neck, moaned and wriggled.

"Welcome home, Terry. HeeHEE, heeHEE!" Nellie Empey called. The table held Nellie's cinnamon rolls, lemonade, and a chocolate pie.

Duffy broke away and ran to me.

"Hi, boy." I wanted to tell him things I'd saved up in my heart—I hadn't had a chance to talk to him since he'd saved my life. But Ma, Dad, and Nellie stood looking at us. I knelt and let Duffy lick my chin.

Dad read my mind. "Your ma has already cried a creek over that dog, and heaped praises on him," he said.

"When my feet are better, we'll go for a walk, just the two of us," I whispered to Duffy.

"*This* time, take your coat," Nellie told me. "HeeHEE, heeHEE."

Dr. Lewis had ordered me to stay off my feet for two weeks. During that time, Duffy lay beside my bed while I read books and magazines, or curled up beside the sofa when I watched TV.

Mom and Linda took Duffy out for walks on a leash, but I could tell he was getting restless. I longed for the day the two of us could get out.

In only ten days, the swelling went down and my toes showed some normal pink color. One morning after Ma had left to go shopping, I found a pair of Dad's old sandals, put them on, and walked around the block. It felt so good to get out, I hardly noticed my feet.

Next day, I searched the sky for clouds. Then Duffy and I started for the foothills. When we reached the outskirts of town, Duffy bounded off, jumping fallen logs, sniffing at animal holes, and chasing ground squirrels.

I had to stop often to rest, and every time I did Duffy returned, sat down beside me, and peered up at my face with solemn, red-brown eyes.

It was a long time before we turned into the Wingates' driveway. Roma, sitting on the front porch knitting, jumped up when she saw me. She hurried into the house, and a moment later I could hear her yelling from her back step.

"*Skiii-nee! Terry's here!*" She picked up a big metal spoon and clanked it on the dinner gong.

She reappeared on the front porch.

"My land, Terry, here you are up and around. Come in the house, out of this heat, and have some juice." She opened the door for Duffy, too.

From the kitchen window I could see Skinny trotting up on his gray horse.

"You didn't have to call Skinny in."

"Why, I did! He's wanted to come to town to see you, but that man has *so* many headaches this time of year. Bringing sheep down from the high country, shipping lambs, sorting ewes. He comes home for a meal, then goes out and works till midnight."

Skinny ducked his head to come in the back door.

"How ya feelin'?" Skinny asked. "I heard they were thinkin' about takin' off your hind feet."

"I still got 'em." I lifted up a sandaled foot.

"Ain't that fine?" he said.

"I wanted to say thank you, for rescuing me."

"A lot of luck involved. Luck and that dog there."

He cocked his head toward Duffy.

Something outside the kitchen window had caught Duffy's attention, and he stood with his back to us, ears perked, front paws on the windowsill.

"Look at that," Roma said. "He sees those sheep clear out there."

I looked out the window. On the rise behind the house, a herder on a brown horse and a band of sheep were barely visible.

Duffy, ears working, yelped.

"Be quiet, Duffy," I said.

Duffy ran to the back door. "Woof!" he barked. He looked at me, wriggled, and whined.

"No, Duffy," I said.

Skinny said, "If you want to open that door and let Duffy run up there with Manuel, he won't hurt nothin'. I'm sure he'd be real hel—"

Roma frowned and shook her head at Skinny.

Duffy ran to me, peered at me with serious eyes, and ran back to the door.

"Could you stay and have some roast with us, Terry?" Roma asked.

"Woof!" Duffy called to the sheep on the hill. *"Woof!"*

"I'd like to, but it looks like I better get Duffy home."

When we got outside, I grabbed hold of Duffy's collar. He fought me, pawing the air and moaning. I needed to get him out of sight and scent of Skinny's place.

I hobbled up the rutted driveway, struggling with my squirming dog. When we reached the Wingates' mailbox, I finally turned loose of him. "Now," I told him, "we'll go over on the lava ridge and you can run your legs off. I can find a stick to throw and . . ." I looked down and Duffy was gone. Even before I turned and looked, I knew he was racing to the hillside where the sheep were.

I cut across the pasture, limping on my sore feet. "Duffy!" I yelled. "Don't! Come here!"

He stopped and looked back, ears working. "I can't run after you, Duffy!" I hollered. "You come right now."

I thought he was going to mind. But just then the herder rode forward into the band, starting to move the sheep to water at the creek. Duffy saw the swirl of white sheep, and bolted up the hillside.

My feet hurt too much to chase after him. I slumped down on an aspen log and waited. I was pretty sure Duffy wouldn't do anything to make the herder or Skinny mad.

I waited a long time. Every now and then, I could see a black-and-white streak in the distance tearing around a moving mass of white-wooled sheep. When I'd almost given up on him coming back, I looked up and saw my dog trotting down the hill.

His ears and tail waved like banners and his nose poked up like he was king of the meadow. Until he saw me watching him. Then he tucked in his tail and dropped his nose. He began to sidle toward me, eyes down. His head hung awkwardly against his chest. When he got near, he whimpered.

I'd been kind of touchy since my adventure on the mountain, and watching Duffy wither up like that brought me to sudden tears.

"I'm not going to scold you," I told him. I reached out my hand. Duffy edged close, his white-tipped tail dragging.

"Let's go home," I said.

Walking back, I had to hobble on overtired feet. But Duffy followed even slower, his tail carving a track in the dust.

CHAPTER SEVENTEEN

Duffy whined at the kitchen door. When I opened it and let him out he raced in circles, sniffing at the ground.

"First he wants in, then he wants out," Ma complained. "Why is he so restless?"

"Not enough exercise the past couple of weeks," I said, worrying it was more than that. Duffy had been acting strange ever since we'd visited the Wingates' the day before.

Suddenly, Duffy sailed over the back gate. He dashed down the alley and out of sight before I could get outside to tell him to stop.

Ma, washing dishes and looking out the window, hollered, "Terence! The dog! Go get him. No, you can't run yet. *I'll* go get him." She thudded to the door. "No! I'm too slow. Go get in the car."

Ma drove the streets in our neighborhood while both of us called out the window, *"Duffy! Here, Duffy!"* We tried downtown, then slowly drove up and down all the streets we hadn't checked. At last I said, "Ma. Try the road to the Wingates'."

We bounced over the rutted road, straining for a glimpse of the dog. Ma's forehead wrinkled with worry.

"It would be bad if he's loose out here, Terence. He could get hit by a car or truck. Of if he gets in some stranger's sheep, he might get shot."

"No!" I protested. But she was right. Ranchers sometimes did shoot strange dogs, because strays could do a lot of harm to their flocks.

Finally we saw Duffy ahead of us, dashing across a rocky foothill. Ma stopped the car. I got out, cupped my hands, and called, *"Duffy!"* Duffy stopped, looked, and raced down the hill to us.

"You scamp!" Ma scolded. "Give us a scare like that." Duffy wagged his tail, lifted his nose to be petted, and jumped into the car. "What's gotten into him, Terence?"

"We went to see Skinny yesterday, and he got excited about the sheep."

"Sheep? Why, he ought to be happy he lives in town. Those ranch dogs work like . . . like . . ." She searched for a word to replace *dogs.*

"It's in his blood, Ma."

"Don't sound annoyed at me, Terence."

Even though Duffy had seemed glad to see us, he acted far away on the ride back to town. He rested his chin on the seat and stared out the back window, ears flat against his head.

At home, Ma said, "You may have to chain him

whenever you let him outside. If you think he's apt to run off again."

I figured he would take off if he got a chance. And the idea of having to watch him every second made me feel like a jailer. All I could hope was that this mood of his would pass.

I took the stout chain Ma had bought, wrapped it around the base of our maple tree, and clipped the heavy hook to Duffy's collar. "You've got a good home here," I told him. "Get those sheep out of your head!"

Within the hour Duffy was barking. Not at anything in particular, just sitting on his hind end with his snout in the air, barking. "Quiet!" Ma yelled to him. Duffy slunk behind the tree.

I brought him inside to sit with me while I watched TV. Ma gave Duffy a saucer of leftover tapioca. It was a warm afternoon, and before long I fell asleep on the rug. Next thing I knew, I heard moaning. I looked up, blinking, and saw Duffy scraping the living room floor in front of the door with his front paws. He was whimpering.

"Cut it out!" I hissed. Duffy was putting scratches on the wood.

"Duffy. Come here," I ordered. "Look, boy, you've got to straighten up. When I go back to school, you'll be by yourself a lot more. You've got a neat deal, living here. Everybody in the family is crazy about you." Duffy gazed at my face with thoughtful red-brown eyes. "You may wish for something else, but ... but ..." I stopped. I had started to tell Duffy I knew what was best for him, but that sounded like Ma used to, when she was arguing I should stay in the choir. And this wasn't the same at all. Of course owners could decide what was best for their dogs.

Duffy tilted his head and looked at me. His eyes were more than serious. They were sad.

"Ma!" I called. "Make Duffy stay in the house, okay?"

I strode down the front walk, turned left, and headed down the hill. I needed to go someplace and think.

CHAPTER EIGHTEEN

I pulled open the heavy door of the church. A scent hung in the air, probably from incense, but maybe the pines beside the building were letting out their breaths.

My sandals clicked on the cold tiles until they were suddenly silent on the carpeted aisle. My fingers found the holy water font, and I touched wet fingers to my forehead, my stomach, one shoulder, then the other. I bent back and looked at the heavy ceiling beams, then swiveled my head side to side to gaze at the pictures in the stained-glass windows and carved figures on the Stations of the Cross. Empty of people, the church seemed strange.

I slipped into a pew. I started to kneel, but instead I slid along the bench, all the way to the end. My jeans whined against the wood. I slid back the other way, smiling at the sound.

Why had I come here? I put my elbow on the arm of the pew and leaned over to rest my cheek on my hand. The denim of my jeans, soft from many washings, bunched up in ridges at my thighs. I poked at the ridges with my finger.

When I looked up again, I stared at the face of the Blessed Mother. Her plaster head tilted to one side and her eyes, even without eyeballs, seemed to gaze at the floor. She held the baby Jesus in the crook of her arm, and He faced the other way, so I couldn't see His expression. Candles in front of the statue flared and then shrunk. Staring at them made me blink.

Ma always lit candles to pray—for wishes, usually, like that a sick person would get better, that someone who died would go to heaven, that the mines would stay open.

I stared at the tilted head, the bent arm holding the baby, the plaster folds of the Blessed Mother's dress, the candles stretching yellow flames above their holders. I stood up, bowed my head to the altar, and took a step toward the statue. I pulled my hand out of my pocket and reached in the direction of the taper used to light candles. But my legs wouldn't go forward. I backed up and sat down again.

I wanted to go light a candle. But then I'd want to ask God to make Duffy into a different kind of dog, one who only wanted to be my pet, and I couldn't pray for that because Duffy was what he was, and I loved him for what he was, and some things are already the way they are supposed to be and shouldn't be changed, and Duffy was one of those things. And then—I knew what I had to do.

So I stayed in the church awhile watching the tilted head, the eyes that looked at the floor, the erupting candles, and the ridges on my jeans darkening with tears.

I was glad Ma was gone when I got home. I strode to the phone before I lost my courage, and called Skinny Wingate.

CHAPTER NINETEEN

If he follows me, I thought, I won't leave him here.

If he wants to come home, I won't force him to stay and be a ranch dog. That was my plan as I walked up the hill toward the Wingates' ranch.

Duffy trotted beside me. He dashed off to chase a bee, then a meadowlark. I slogged up the slope.

Duffy's ears started to flick and his tail waved behind his body. He had spied a band of ewes on the adjoining hillside.

Skinny Wingate strode toward me, that floating walk of his gobbling up ground. He pushed his cowboy hat off his forehead when I got near and stood and waited for me. His gaze swept over the dog, admiring as always, but his eyes rested on my face.

"You're doin' right," he said.

I nodded. I'd explained everything on the phone, because I knew I wouldn't be able to talk then. My words, like my heart, would be all broken. I'd tried to put a rim of ice around my feelings before I left town, but it wasn't working, and I knew it must show on my face. One thing I wouldn't do was cry, not in front of this big rancher.

Wingate looked at me sidelong.

"Didn't change your mind?" It was a question, but there was a statement in it too. I shook my head and looked at the ground.

"Come here," the deep voice said. I looked up, startled, but I saw Skinny was talking to Duffy. My beautiful border collie, whose black hair spilled over one eye like melted licorice, trotted over to Skinny Wingate. He stared up at the towering rancher with serious, red-brown eyes. I believe he knew he was going to work.

"You're doin' right," Wingate said again. A crackle in the words startled me. Then I saw something I never in my life expected to see. Skinny Wingate's eyes held tears. Wingate flicked a thumb over his leathery cheek, told the dog, "C'mon," turned, and glided up the hill toward the ewes.

If the dog turns around and wants to come with me, I told myself, I'll let him. If Skinny Wingate has to call Duffy, because Duffy really wants to go home with me, that will change things. I was walking across the meadow, stepping over prickly pear plants and plucking straws of crested wheat. I glanced over my shoulder. Duffy was not coming. He was running, in a half crouch, toward the sheep.

I hated him then. Sure, I'd told Skinny Wingate I'd give him the dog, but only a part of me had believed I'd have to do it. In the movies, the dog would have lingered on the hillside, barked after me, then raced to catch me. He would have jumped up on my legs to tell me he really would be happy as a town dog after all. I'd come prepared to let go of my dog. But I'd hoped my dog wouldn't be able to let go of me.

When I reached the rise on the gravel road, I hesitated. I would be torturing myself to turn around. But I couldn't resist. After the rise, the road fell toward town and I would be out of sight and so would Duffy.

I peeked back. And there, just like in the movies, he stood, skylined on the brow of the hill, watching me.

I waved, grinning until my face ached. "C'mon, boy!" I called. "Sure. Come on!"

Duffy began to move down the hill toward me. Slowly. He placed each foot warily, like he was dodging quicksand, and his white-tipped tail trailed in the dust. Fact was, his hind end dragged like a dog who'd been injured.

He inched down the slope, his head cranking around to gaze behind him to the ridge. I couldn't stand it.

"No, Duffy," I called. "Stop!"

Duffy stopped.

"Stay!" I ordered, and held up my palm.

Duffy sat. He cocked his head. I turned and started off again, my chin tucked into my shirt collar. "Stay!" I muttered, the words bouncing off my chest.

From the grassy slope beyond the gorge, Skinny Wingate's whistle pierced the air. I took the biggest steps I could down the hill. I stared at the roadbed and my sandaled feet slapping at pebbles, dust pockets, and scurrying ants. But I didn't see them.

I saw Duffy—beside me at a trout stream, rolling on the backyard grass with me, walking on his hind legs outside the hospital window.

I knew if I stopped, the rock in my chest would move up to my throat and cut off my breathing. So I hurried, head down, gulping air, and wondering if it would always hurt this bad.

CHAPTER TWENTY

"Terry," Dad said. "C'mon, let's go fishing."

I shook my head.

"For heaven's sake, take him!" Ma scowled. "If you have to drag him."

I pushed my hands deeper into my pockets and stared at the floor. It had been a week since I'd given Duffy to Skinny Wingate. When I'd first told Ma and Dad about it, Ma had bawled her eyes out. But after that, she'd jumped into a crusade to distract me with food. She'd served chicken and homemade noodles for supper twice, and every night after we'd finished washing the dishes, a beautiful dessert appeared on the table.

"You've hardly set foot outside," Dad said. "School starts on Tuesday and we don't know how many warm Saturdays we'll have before the snows hit." Dad had given me lots of invitations to go places with him. Mostly, I'd turned him down.

"I'm fed up with this moping," Ma declared. She placed squares of chocolate in a saucepan to melt and said to Dad, "Maybe he needs a pie."

"Terry." Dad plunked down beside me on the sofa.

"No," I said.

"Before you got Duffy, you fished without him."

"It's different now," I said.

It was odd. Sometimes, for just a minute, I'd feel like my old self. Then I'd see a dog running down the street, my bucket platform sitting in the corner of my closet, or the red Frisbee lying on the porch, and sadness would overcome me again.

Ma put her fists on her hips. "I could always find a chore for you, Terence, if you won't go fishing. Maybe you'd like to scrub the kitchen floor?"

I shrugged. It made no difference to me what I did.

Skinny had called once, to say Duffy was doing great. "You come on out and visit him as often as you want," he'd said.

"No, thank you," I'd told him. Seeing Duffy, and knowing he was no longer my dog, would be too hard.

Dad said, "I did Nellie Empey's lawn yesterday. But she wants you back. She loves to have a boy around to bake for."

"Okay, I'll go see her sometime." My voice sounded flat.

Ma thudded over. "Get your hands out of your pockets, Terence. It makes you look like riffraff."

She leaned on the sofa arm, peered into my face, and said to Dad, "Maybe when he was layin' out in the snow, it froze up his wits." She pinched my cheek. I didn't know how she could even try to joke around.

"Terence, you always could go back to choir," Dad said. "Father would—"

"Just leave me alone!" I stalked out of the house and down the front steps, stumbling a bit on the stairs.

I walked past Miner's Park and the dirt airstrip and headed up the path to Wild Horse Creek. My toes felt almost normal, except when I stepped on a sharp rock—then pain shot up my leg.

I found a boulder and sat down beside the creek. Grass that had blanketed the banks in June had dried up and blown away, and the creek, which used to roar downhill, now trickled over the rock shelf. I leaned over to peer into a deep, green pool to see if I could spy any fish. The pool looked empty.

I thought about how much I had lost: Duffy, seeing Vic every day at choir practice, and the scholarship. Giving up Duffy had been the right thing, though; I was sure of that. And letting the scholarship go to a boy who really planned to study music was the right thing too.

I hiked up a hillside. At the top of the slope, I

lay down on my stomach beside a bubbling spring and took a big gulp of water. *Don't drink from springs, Terence,* I could hear my mother scold. *They're not safe anymore. You want a case of giardiasis?* The water tasted wonderful.

My eye at that level spied a bush of wild raspberries, ripe for picking. I plucked off red fruits, no bigger than the end of my finger, and ate them one at a time, letting their sweetness fill my mouth. I closed my eyes and chewed, thinking they were the best thing I'd ever tasted.

I found another bush with berries, sat down to eat, and watched the sun float in and out of wispy clouds. About twenty feet away, a five-point buck deer, still in velvet, glided through the aspens. I felt an ache. Duffy would have been excited; he always loved seeing wildlife.

I was trying to swallow around the log wedged in my throat when, out of the blue, a thought struck me. Duffy was now doing what he was meant to do. And someday I, Terry Riley, would find out what I was meant to do with my life. When I found it, I'd know it inside, just like Duffy had known.

I ambled home. It looked so different, with the heavy undergrowth gone. Some of my favorite things hadn't changed, though. A heavy mint scent still hung over the road, white sego lilies bloomed in the meadow, and ground squirrels scurried and scolded. One thing was new. The raspberries. They came at the end of summer.

I went home and went to bed early. But before I fell asleep, I heard voices in the living room. Ma tapped on my door, then peeked in.

"Terence, company to see you."

"Who?" My heart pounded. A deep voice from the living room sounded like Skinny Wingate's. What if he'd brought Duffy to visit? It would rip open my wounds.

"Is Duffy. . . ?"

Ma, mouth tight, shook her head.

I pulled on my clothes and shuffled to the living room. Inside my jeans pocket, I crossed my fingers. Had something happened with Duffy that would make Skinny want to bring him back?

"Terry." Skinny crossed the room and shook my hand. Roma blinked. "Terry," she said.

Skinny ran his hands around the brim of his cowboy hat.

"Sit down," Dad said.

"Coffee?" Ma asked.

"Please," Skinny said.

Skinny's knees poked up from the sofa. He pursed his mouth and looked at Roma. Roma jerked her head at Skinny. Dad looked from one to the other.

"So, how's the sheep business, Skinny? Lamb prices good?"

Skinny nodded. "They're good." He scowled at the rug. Roma gave him a poke.

Skinny coughed. "Terry, me and Roma want to . . . talk to you about somethin'." Roma smiled.

"That dog of yours is sure enough doin' a good job for us, Terry. Haven't had one like 'im since Cody died. Pug Peters come by and watched Duffy the other day, and sure did praise 'im."

Skinny took a mug of coffee from Ma.

"Pug and some of the other ranchers want to have pups from him. They're going to bring us their bitches to breed to him."

Was Skinny going to offer me the money he made using Duffy as a stud dog?

I put up my hand. "You keep any money you get from that," I said.

Roma looked startled. "My land, Terry, we don't charge anybody to breed their dogs. I pray to God we're never so poor we can't help people get good dogs."

I flushed, feeling stupid.

"But we *are* here to have a conversation about . . . money," Skinny said. He scratched his forehead.

I froze. Surely Skinny would realize I couldn't take any money for Duffy.

"That dog of yours, Terry, is going to improve

the quality of stock dogs in this valley. And everybody sure does appreciate it. Me and Roma the
most.

"Now, I know he was your friend, and we can't
give you nothin' that would touch the value of
him. But we been thinkin' . . ." He glanced at
Roma.

"Me 'n' Roma never was fortunate enough to
have kids of our own. Roma always put away the
money she made sewing dresses and drapes for
people so we could send our children to college.
But you can see"—Skinny pointed to his gray hair
"—ain't likely we'll have those kids we were an-
ticipatin'.

"That money's earned interest in the bank, and
there's a bit of it now. About twelve hundred fifty
dollars. We sure would be proud to see it go to
help educate another child." Skinny took a swig
of coffee, hiding his face.

Roma looked at Ma. "We hope this don't insult
you, Maggie and John. We know you provide
good for Terry, but with the mine so unpredict-
able . . ."

Dad blinked. Ma's mouth hung open. And of
course, Ma couldn't hear an offer like that without her eyes clouding over. But she was proud.
She would turn it down.

"Ma," I spoke up. "Next summer I could get
more lawn jobs. Then the next summer I'd be old

enough to work on a farm or ranch. If I added the money I made summers to the Wingates' money . . ."

Ma looked at me, stunned. It was the most words I'd said in a week.

"I could go to college, Ma."

"It would make us so happy," Roma said. "Kind of comfort us in our disappointment."

"Roma," Ma gasped. "That's the most generous thing I ever heard of."

Roma hauled herself off the sofa and marched over to me.

"That's not so, Maggie. The most generous thing I ever did hear of was this boy givin' up that dog."

The Wingates insisted, Ma resisted, but finally it was agreed I could accept their gift. After they left, it began to sink in. I found that inside myself, I wanted something that Ma wanted for me. I wanted to go to college. I wanted to have an occupation more dependable than Dad's.

And this way, I could pick what I wanted to study. I could be a forest ranger. Or a pharmacist. Or an archaeologist. Maybe I'd even study music. I'd have a choice.

I found Dad in the kitchen, washing up the coffee cups.

"Would tomorrow morning work for going fishing?"

Dad looked up and grinned. "You bet," he said. "And hey, after our bills are paid, you'd accept contributions to your college fund, wouldn't you?"

The next day we went to early Mass. Then Dad and I loaded our poles and drove up to Manzanita Creek. I missed Duffy being there. But the fish were biting good, and Dad and I both caught our limits.

Ma had sent along fat chicken sandwiches with Swiss cheese and lettuce, and fresh lemonade in a thermos. Dad and I climbed to the rim above the creek and ate lunch on a rock table.

An eagle screamed above us. We chewed our sandwiches, watching the bird float on a thermal. Early frost had killed the flies. Maple bushes on the hill flashed red and the quakies quivered with gold.

Heading back to the creek, Dad leaned over to sniff a patch of yellow flowers. Cold had nipped them and their petals sagged.

"I wandered lonely as a cloud," I said, "that floats on high o'er vales and hills . . ."

Dad, brows furrowed, looked up at me. "What's that?"

"A poem we used to say in choir.

> *. . . When all at once I saw a crowd,*
> *A host of golden daffodils;*
> *Beside the lake, beneath the trees,*
> *Fluttering and dancing in the breeze."*

"These aren't daffodils," Dad said.

"I know," I said. "They're heart-leafed arnica. Nellie Empey says the flowers make a salve. Maybe I should take her some."

I stretched out my hand to pluck them. Their fragrance reached my nose.

"Maybe I'll leave them here," I said.

Dad stood up, breathed deep, and gazed at the range above us. "So what's the rest of the poem about the flowers?"

"I can't remember the middle verses. The last one goes,

> *For oft, when on my couch I lie*
> *In vacant or in pensive mood,*
> *They flash upon that inward eye*
> *Which is the bliss of solitude;*
> *And then my heart with pleasure fills,*
> *And dances with the daffodils."*

"I like poems," Dad said. "I wish I understood them better. You understand that one?"

I shrugged. "I didn't used to. And I don't know what it means to anybody else. To me it means, if you come across something neat, it will always be yours. Nothing can take it away, because, you know, you have the memory."

Dad looked at me hard.

"That's how it is with Duffy and me," I said. "I'll always like remembering."